FALLING THROUGH THE CRACKS

Stories By

Julio Ricci

Translated by Clark M. Zlotchew

WHITE PINE PRESS

©1989 Julio Ricci (original stories)
Translations ©1989 Clark Zlotchew

ISBN 0-934834-25-3

Acknowledgements

   The Spanish originals of these stories appeared in the following books:
   "The Letter" ("La carta") and "The Mantle of Command" ("La jerarquia") are from *Cuentos Civilizados* (Montevideo: Ediciones Geminis, 1985).
   "Mr. Szomogy's Best Friend" ("Las amistades del Sr. Szomogy") and "The Loser" ("El desubicado") are from *Ocho modelos de felicidad* (Buenos Aires: Macondo Ediciones, 1980).
   "Old Friends" ("El Shoijet") is from *El Grongo* (Montevideo: Ediciones Geminis, 1976).
   "The Table" ("La mesita") is from *Los maniaticos* (Montevideo: Editorial Alfa, 1970).
   "The Concert" ("El concierto") is from *Los mareados: Cuentiario* (Montevideo: Monte Sexto, 1987).

English translations of some of these stories have appeared in the *Webster Review* and the *New Orleans Review*.

Publication of this book was made possible, in part, by grants from the National Endowment for the Arts and the New York State Council on the Arts.

Design by Watershed Design.

WHITE PINE PRESS
P.O. Box 236
Buffalo, New York 14201

76 Center Street
Fredonia, New York 14063

CONTENTS

ABOUT JULIO RICCI...

In a modest house in a quiet, middle-class neighborhood, he sits at the table with his wife Iris and me, the same table at which we just had dinner—courtesy of Iris. He does more than merely answer my questions: he communicates with me in an open and frank manner about literature, about life, about the human condition, about friendship and love, about the inexorable passage of time which is responsible for aging, death, and the loss of those dear to him.

Julio Ricci, a rare personality, combines a scientific mind with humanity and art. This urban Uruguayan, born in Montevideo in 1921, received his degree in Spanish language and Hispanic literatures from the Instituto de Estudios Superiores. He has spent most of his life studying and teaching linguistics—a highly technical subject involving the grammatical and phonological structures of language—and learning foreign languages. He has studied and taught in Sweden, Italy, France, and the United States, and, until his recent retirement from the Instituto Nacional de Docencia in the city of his birth, devoted his life to the linguistic preparation of his nation's teachers.

Ricci admits that linguistics began to seem overly scientific,

1

coldly inhuman and computerized. As a balance to this technical field, he enjoyed reading fiction, especially that of Eastern Europe. Finally, he felt the overwhelming need to create his own fictional world, a world into which he pours his humanitarian concerns, his keen observation, his active imagination, his psychological insight, and his love for the human race. All this leavened by a unique sense of humor—at times wry, at times hearty—which not only tempers his fiction but which radiates from him, spontaneously flowing from the after-dinner conversation.

Ricci has been the object of increasing attention in recent years. His collections of short fiction include *Los maniáticos* (1970), *El Grongo* (1976), *Ocho modelos de felicidad* (1980), *Cuentos civilizados* (1985), and *Los mareados* (1987). He has received seven first prize awards for his fiction, six in Uruguay. A seventh was recently given for the collection *Cuentos civilizados* by the Argentinian magazine *Entre Todos*. His winning this prize in a Latin America-wide competition is comparable to a Canadian author's receiving first prize in a contest open to writers from the entire English-speaking world.

The popularity and universality of Ricci's work is attested to by the translation of many of his stories into Italian, French, German, Portuguese, English, Polish, Russian, and Bulgarian, although this present collection is the first anthology of his narratives to be published in any language other than Spanish. His growing importance in Uruguayan letters can be glimpsed in his work being the subject of an entire session at the Colloquium on French/Uruguayan Cultural Relations sponsored by the Sorbonne and held at UNESCO headquarters in Paris in December 1987.

Ricci's fiction often involves the grim, grey, at times hopeless lives of realistic, even crude, characters who represent various types of social outcasts, misfits, and grotesques living on the fringes of society in a Montevideo which has lost its former ebullience. Yet within the anodine, routine lives of ordinary Montevideans, against the backdrop of the totally normal and recognizable atmosphere of the Uruguayan capital, there reigns, as Hugo Verani put it, the absurd as a way of life presented, as Oscar Satinosky notes, with huge doses of black humor. While recognizing these elements in Ricci's work, Fernando Ainsa also refers to a vision of life "steeped in poetry and magic." Italian critic Giovanni Meo Zilio affirms that a feature common to all Ricci's narratives is "poetic language (common to the language of dreams)" as well as a certain "theatricality." Indeed, much of the charm of Ricci's stories stems precisely from his talent for using an unmistakable, concrete Montevideo, with its true street names and neighborhoods, as the foundation for an ineffably poetic and magical space.

In some stories, Ricci's characters are grotesque, even despicable, while in others they are obviously the object of the author's warm affection. Yet in all the stories, no matter how savage or bitter, his great sympathy toward his characters, toward the human race, is plainly in evidence. Perhaps the single element that makes all Ricci's personages—and all human beings— so dear to him, in spite of their faults, is their very mortality.

Ricci has always believed his writing to be concerned basically with social criticism; nevertheless, I suggested to him that perhaps it was not only societal problems that interested him but also—and for me, predominantly—the relationships established between individuals and the way in which time alters these relationships. Ricci thought for a moment and answered:

"Exactly. What shakes me to the core, what hurts me most, is to see how fleeting time is. That woman I met [the inspiration for the story "The Letter"], I saw her for only ten minutes, and then ten years later I find a piece of paper with her address on it, but I don't see her anymore. She has disappeared; this person is no longer part of my life. All the fragments of our lives disappear bit by bit, and we can't hold on to them. This is a frightful thing. For me it's a tragedy. My friend Bordoli sat at this very table at which you and I are seated now. So did my friend Garini, my friend Botto, my friend González— writers, friends—and they've already died, disappeared. And there's nothing that can be done about it. It's a terrible feeling, one of great anguish, to see

3

people with whom we've had this great affinity, this great friendship and great affection, disappear completely from our lives."

It is not that Ricci is preoccupied with death; it is his love of life, his respect and affection for each individual human being—all the more precious in his consciousness through his realization of the individual's irreplaceable uniqueness—that infuses all his work. Perhaps this accounts for the warm reception the stories have received. Uruguayan critic Martha L. Canfield noted that Ricci's characters "are, more than anything else, poor creatures at the mercy of death. As we all are. This is why the reader easily identifies with them; this is why they move him to compassion, beyond their ridiculous or caricaturesque aspects."

Routine plays a great part in Ricci's fiction. The constant hour-by-hour, day-by-day, year-by-year repetition of certain acts: arising, having coffee and toast, taking the bus along the same route every day, seeing the same four walls at the office, filling out the same forms, taking the bus home along the same route, going to bed at the same hour. Routine, felt as a soul-deadening presence in many of Ricci's stories, is at times viewed as something comfortable, even precious, by some of his characters. This ambivalence is not contradictory: routine gives the impression of stopping time. It appears to make the present last forever and to fend off death and the loss of dear ones. In fact, there are those whose lives are so empty—devoid of love, of friendship, even of creature comforts—that routine has become the sole entity on which they can depend, holding meaning and permanence for them. Without the financial capacity for material goods, lacking the emotional support of friends and lovers, these lost souls would be completely adrift were it not for the stabilizing element of daily routine. For these unfortunate people, stultifying routine becomes a substitute for the elements missing from their lives.

The concept of routine as a bulwark against a hostile world and a substitute for love leads us to the common theme underlying the superficially varied situations in Ricci's fiction: loneliness. At the top of Ricci's scale of values are love and friendship, but his characters find these to be precious, and all

4

too rare, commodities. The absence of these comforts is what makes them fall victim to solitude, a condition which, in turn, converts them into grotesques, with peculiar quirks and manias, who live in silence and desperation and fall through the cracks of the societal structure.

It is notable that while many of Ricci's short stories deal with native-born Montevideans, a significantly high proportion of them revolve around people born in Eastern Europe or the Middle East. This is only partially explicable in terms of his literary preferences. These tales are populated by Poles, Hungarians, Ukrainians, Russian Jews, Turkish Jews, and Armenians. In fact, in would be possible to divide Ricci's fiction into two branches: that concerning the drab, monotonous world of native Uruguayans frustrated by an impersonal bureaucracy operating under a military dictatorship, and that involving the equally desperate, equally hopeless—at times sordid, at times sumptuous—world that extends from Russia and Poland, passes through the Balkans, and ends in Turkey. The inhabitants of this enchanted region suffer as much as, if not more than, the native- born Uruguayans, but they have another dimension to their lives, a dimension of profound interest to Ricci. This magical region is Ricci's refuge from the dystopia of the impersonal, technologically advanced modern world—Ricci's West—into the poetry of a world which is still as human, and as magical, as he imagines the West of his youth was. Unable to travel in time, Ricci's narrators travel in space and transmute time—the golden age of Ricci's youth—into space: a utopian geographical region to the east and southeast of Europe.

Perhaps Domingo Luis Bordoli's comment is of the greatest relevance to the prospective reader: "One definite effect produced by his stories: one doesn't forget them."

—C.M.Z.

FALLING THROUGH
THE CRACKS

THE CONCERT

I've just thoroughly rinsed my mouth with a liquid that came highly recommended to me and which really soothes my throat. I'm sure that some of my friends are doing the same thing at this very moment. Friends? What friends...? I hardly even know them! They're a bunch of senior citizens even older than I am, or a bunch of old folks even more senior than I am, who sit next to me on those broken-down chairs that are almost black with age, and laugh without knowing why.

Obviously, times change and technology is creating new and previously unimagined professions. Carpentry, blacksmithing, tailoring and so many other biblical trades will soon disappear. In the future, readers of the Bible will have to take special courses to understand these things.

Well, maybe what my contemporaries and I do doesn't constitute a trade or a profession. It is an as-yet unnamed activity performed by people like us who can't do anything else any longer. Or rather, by people like us who can't do anything more than demand almost nothing as pay and accept the crumbs they throw us.

I must confess that there was a time when I was impressed by the phrase from a tango: "… and not think about myself any more." I was impressed because at that time, and until very recently, I'd actually stopped thinking about myself. Just like everyone else. Who stops to think about himself? What you think about is your daily problems, but not yourself. That's the luxury of philosophers.

Yesterday I laughed a lot, which is not the same as saying I had a good laugh. However, the director told us our output was poor, that we had to produce heartier laughs and louder guffaws. He informed us that he had made a computerized market survey and that the computer had indicated that the stronger the laughter, the greater the audience stimulation, the greater the comedian's success, and the greater the television channel's profits.

He didn't say a word about raising our salaries even ten cents. The minimum wage was sufficient; this seemed to be the tacit statement. What he did say was that we would do well to protect our positions. In other words, he threatened us.

It's been horribly cold since last week, and I find it hard to get up early, wash, shave and have my coffee. Those cold blasts whipping up out of Patagonia are bad for my health. At the bus stop I have to stand there shivering and trying to breathe in the face of some really fierce winds. By the time the bus comes along I'm stiff with cold.

The six hours of work at the T.V. station are exhausting. Who would imagine that while so many people work with their hands or their brains, others do it—we do it—with laughter. That's right: we sell laughs. No one would imagine that laughs, yuks, are today a marketable product, that there is a laugh market and that this market even has its prices quoted on the stock exchange. A little while ago I wouldn't have thought that at this stage of my life—I've seen seventy-four Christmases come and go— I would end up in this profession. It's only the simple exercise, or the simple exploitation, of a condition natural to man. (An animal would never make a living on laughter.)

The director informed us that on May 10 the channel would present a comedian of great international renown—a Julio Iglesias or a Pelé or a Ronald Reagan of the joke and the pun—

and that we had to be prepared to laugh "mightily," and, if possible, to duly prolong our peals of laughter, like the great tenors, I suppose. He told us he had even hired back-up laughter personnel, and that he was going to test their abilities. He said that if they turn out to be better than we are, we'll be relieved of our duties.

Perhaps as a result of this employment or, para-employment, I often find myself thinking about myself. The truth is that the pettiness of life, the narrowness of daily routine—getting up and lying down, eating, earning a living, defecating, in other words, all those things that parade before our senses daily— distract attention from our innermost selves and inhibit us from thinking. I've always lived wrapped up in those things, perhaps like Rockefeller, like Reagan, like the Pope, always organizing "exteriorities": the world banking crisis, the struggles for democracy, social contacts, etc. And I've given very little time to thinking about my own nothingness.

The day before yesterday the elderly laugher sitting next to me was feeling ill. He had launched a volley of hoarse, peculiar peals of laughter and then suddenly passed out: he deflated, you might say, and fell to the floor. They left him there a while, stretched out on the floor. His eyes were closed. It was not possible to interrupt the comedian. The block of time, more important than the old man, had to be filled. The director had him placed on a stretcher immediately after the time was up.

"Get that old man out of here," he said.

He was taken away and immediately replaced by a substitute who was equally old, but uglier and almost a dwarf. Nothing more was ever heard of the other man. He was history and had no importance. The show—that is, the present—had to go on, period. I did notice, however, that the new old man, the dwarf, laughed with enormous stridency. You could tell he had a terrific constitution.

I think that the new practice of calibrating the decibel level of our laughter is going too far. But what can you do! Everything is technified and quantified and paid for these days.

I haven't told anyone about it, but I'm training myself, or simply training, as they say nowadays, at home. I'm trying to increase the volume of my laughter. The truth is that I've never been much of a laugher, let alone someone who would split a gut laughing. In fact, there were those who labeled me as sad. I never thought that one day I would end up, not just doing piecework laughs, but even worrying about my style of laughter, of guffaws, and studying the various types of laughter. And even less that I'd end up classifying them by their duration, their decibel level, their tone. Today I know that there are provocative laughs, laughs which are sexually arousing, ironic laughs, bestial laughs, brutal and even erotic laughs. There is a whole gamut of ways to laugh, and I'm sure that one day German scientists will write the *Treatise on Laughter* or *Grundriss des Lachens*. And the Americans will evaluate them in all their economic and monetary aspects (free floating, basic cash reserves, projected growth, etc.), and the Japanese will commercialize them in the form of calibrating mechanisms and will even manufacture laughing robots.

I'm worried about the arrival of the great comedian from Spain. I foresee that we present laughers will all have to outdo ourselves at that time. We'll have to employ all our ebbing pulmonary strength, stretch our vocal cords to the limit, and put on our most cheerful party faces to keep our jobs.

I've just noticed something that strikes me as odd. They're setting up what looks like traffic lights facing our work area. One of the many bigwigs who come and go at the television station said that these are the lights the director is going to use. Red will mean *silence*; yellow will mean *get ready*; and green will be the signal to burst out laughing. The man doesn't want to have to use his hands anymore.

Lately I've noticed that this job's routine is even changing our personalities. The other day, the director had a word with one of the laughers, old González, seventy-seven years of age. He was entirely serious, pointing out González's faults, and his habit of laughing at the wrong time. The old man, instead of paying attention to the director, agreeing and thanking him, began to laugh uproariously. It was as though his brakes had failed and he couldn't stop. I myself, whenever I go to the store or talk to anyone, can't help laughing. Not even the economic crisis or Denmark's six-to-one soccer victory (I'm a Uruguayan) stops me. I'm conscious of this, so I make a great effort to prevent it. And I turn my face to the side, take out a handkerchief, and pretend to sneeze and cough when I laugh.

I'm impressed, or maybe it would be more accurate to say I am unimpressed, by the behavior of the great comedians. People who see them flaunt themselves and show off in order to produce an atmosphere of merriment and uproar are convinced that these comics are on the ball. They think they're happy-go-lucky, friendly guys who let their hair down and get familiar with everyone and kid around with people. But they're really nothing at all like that. When they arrive, we old folks are already waiting there in our chairs, our laughter at the ready to encourage them, to cheer them on. And out of all these comics, not one ever deigned even to look at us. In fact, we're just like the furniture, the carpets and the other inanimate objects that comprise the set. We're props or even less. When their act is over, they disconnect their jovial faces, plug in their serious faces, and leave, stone-faced, without even glancing at anyone. The comic turns into the anti-comic. Some of them have hellish tempers and will swear like troopers for the least little thing.

The truth is that because it's our job to laugh and to concentrate on our work, we no longer pay any attention to the jokes. Besides, when you become familiar with the whole repertoire of television jokes these comedians have, you realize it's something like one single mold into which some new material is poured. It's basically a sort of mechanical exercise based on puns and crude vulgarities. But people go for all that. They love hearing vulgarities over and over. My colleagues, the "laugh aids," do nothing but wait for the green light (laugh) or the red light (cease laughing) from the director. They've even stopped thinking. Sometimes, and I include myself, it's hard for us to stop laughing. After all, we produce laughter for a period of more than thirty seconds, and we fall victim to inertia. We lose control and keep right on laughing. The director becomes furious and even curses. He has a certain Toscanini-like air about him; all he lacks is talent. In other words, he possesses all the attributes of a great conductor—the balding head, the energy, the seriousness of purpose, the capacity for insult—but no orchestra. Conducting laughter is not the same as conducting the symphony orchestra of a great concert hall. Still, if he

13

were skilled, he'd be able to lend a certain choir-like flavor to the group. But it's obvious that he's not. All he thinks about are the lights, about mechanical things, just as we do.

Yesterday he called me and another laugher over, and told us our laughter had a very low level of resonance. It didn't reach the established decibel level. He threatened to fire us and to take on any one of the ninety candidates (retirees) who are waiting their turn, i.e., are waiting for one of us to die. He lost his temper, shouted and even became disheveled as he waved his arms about like a symphony orchestra conductor, but minus the orchestra.

The fact is that we're all old, or rather a bunch of old folks, which is not the same thing. I don't know why they don't hire young people. The youngest old person is a seventy-two-year-old wraith who weighs no more than 120 pounds. A certain Pérez Galindo or Galindo Pérez. The oldest oldster is an old lady of eighty-two years of age, Doña Juanita.

While we were waiting for the bus, Pérez told me that there are times when he doesn't feel well, that he suffers from heart problems, but that at this stage of the game he can't afford to give up his job because he couldn't live on his retirement income. I don't know how long I can keep it up. Where there's life there's hope. It's all going to depend on my gargling, my training program and, absolutely, on the decibel level of my laughter.

I practice a lot at night. I'm trying to raise the volume of my laughter. I do this in front of the bathroom mirror. I look at myself just as I am when I laugh. It's not like Borges' mirrors, filled with the mysteries of the Kabbala, with gardens of forking paths and with metaphysics. It's a mirror of primary and superficial properties. A mirror that shows how my veins swell, shows a mouth with unsteady false teeth (I can't afford new dentures). It shows the saliva that at times sprays the glass surface. What I really would like would be a mirror that would show the way I looked as a young man. But it hasn't been invented yet. Maybe sometime in the future they'll invent a retrospective, or rather, rejuvenating mirror.

I never imagined the world would come to this degree of competition. At my age I'm like young men competing for careers,

14

building their muscles, etc. I'm sure that in spite of everything I'll improve. I'll turn out bigger and better laughs.

I haven't done badly with this job. I've made new friends and I've broken away from the confines of my little room's four walls. I've launched an incredible social life. Little old Juanita invited me to her room for tea and to witness her different styles of laughter. Well, what else could she invite me to? She gave me a demonstration of laughs in several tones and told me all about the ups and downs of her extensive love life while we had a few cups of tea. She's in pretty good condition despite her age.

Juanita has arrived at this stage of her life with not much to show for it. Well, at a certain point in life, human beings gradually get rid of almost everything. Material goods lose their meaning. The poor woman makes do with very little, as elderly folks do. She has a miniscule bed, a little table with a kerosene stove, a kettle and one chair. The walls are virgin; there's nothing hanging on them. If she were a man, she'd at least have a photo of the Peñarol Soccer Team, or their rival, the Nacional Team, maybe from the thirties, or a photo of Carlos Gardel, the great tango singer of years gone by. But there's nothing there. On a small shelf or bracket—and this is all there is—there are some faded photographs. A man and a woman. And also some prints of the Virgin Mary and of Jesus on the cross. All these things, memories, help her go on with her long life. It was very cold, and Juanita was wrapped in a coat of mangy fur that made me think of the ermine stole in the tango of the same name.

"This profession, if that's the right term, will never become unionized," she commented. "It's a step lower than that of prostitutes, who are already unionized in some countries. Our struggle will always have to be individual. To the death."

"You're right," I agreed.

Don Juan I, there are two other Juans (luckily my name is José) asked me to visit him, too. He wanted to speak to me about the great comedian who'd be coming soon, the Pelé or Julio Iglesias or Sinatra of jokes. The "Messiah of Jokedom," as he called him. He told me how he imagined him to be. He would be a real gentleman, very Spanish, very continental, very kind.

He would shake hands with each and every one of us and would lavish on us his great affection and warmth, the affection and warmth of a great maestro. He wouldn't be like our local comics.

Don Juan I began to speak in great circumlocutions, periphrastically beating around the bush in ever-widening circles until I couldn't tell where he was coming from or where he was heading. Finally, when it was time to leave and I stood up, he ended his conceptual bush beating and his deviosities and managed to say something less muddled. He told me he had a great surprise in store for the comedian.

Once more I looked around at Juan I's miserable little room. Juan I, my contemporary, skinny, ugly, poor and generally beat up. His entire world was composed of two chairs that were falling apart, a bed that was actually a cot, a Bulgarian kerosene stove, a three-legged table that was short and squat, plus a pot, a kettle and the utensils used for brewing and drinking the indispensable *maté*. There wasn't even a guitar anywhere or even cookies on the table, but I did see little bottles of medication and some used corn plasters.

"Yes, I have a great surprise for him," he said, and then burst out with two peals of laughter for practice.

I went downstairs in the dark of the night, almost having to grope my way along, and came to Baldomero Fernández Romero, the street named for the poet, and the corner of either Laguna or Pergamino—I'm not sure which—to take the bus.

The great day arrived. The comic's name was Radamés Dilurio or Delugeo or Diluvian. Just like all his fellow comedians, he didn't even glance at us. We were nothing more than some five hundred or six hundred combined years of veteran or veterinary or vegetable entities installed in rows of chairs. We were preparing our throats and making muffled, indefinable noises. We were tuning up our instruments as musicians do in concert halls. The hum of our vocal cords could be heard in their pre-warm-up state.

Supercomic Dilurio strode forward, Mussolini-like, and plugged in his beaming face, activating the facial muscles that produce the conventional smile mechanisms. He selected one of the faces on his program: that of a pampered idiot. It was obvious he was master of an entire repertoire of facial expressions: we could see this immediately. It ranged from the nuance of a lively fool to that of a hopeless idiot. In other words, he had at his command the entire infinite range of tele-hilarious and tele-sensitive touches. He was a blend of Charlie Chaplin, Sid Caesar, Buster Keaton, Bob Hope, Milton Burlesque, Rodney Dangerfield, and Eddie Murphy. He went from an expression of boredom to one of fatigue, of rage, of joy, of enchantment, of eroticism *con fuoco* à la Red Foxx, and of chaste bashfulness. He went through the entire range with which thirty centuries of theatrical necessity have endowed humanity.

He started his collection of jokes. The whole program was based on famous telegrams. The audience began to laugh, and we started our accompaniment. I had never seen my colleagues so excited. It was like a key soccer match, like a world final or one with a high score between, let's say, Denmark and Uruguay. The ball was passed back and forth, and the people roared with excitement. It was wonderful.

The second batch of jokes started with the kind that could be called pornographic. Jokes, that is, in tune with the times. But it was cybernetic pornography. How would the machines of the future make love? What was the love-making style of Japanese robots? How would computers reproduce?

There was a moment in which Dilurio the Great had all his transistors in operation, his face contorted with eroticism, and everyone's spirits soaring. At this moment Don Juan I stood up, emerged from the obscurity of the laugh team, positioned himself center stage, and began to laugh. The lighting crew, not knowing what was happening, illuminated his face and body in lights of every color. They practically bathed him in color.

Suddenly there was soft music. Don Juan I began to emit peals of laughter. He passed from one type of laughter to another, from a *do*, to a *re*, to a *mi*, and so on. He utilized every nuance imaginable: laughter that was violent, soft, savage, grotesque, intelligent, miniscule, gigantic. He was a complete concert of unimaginable laughter and was such a spectacle that the comedian, the telegrams, the eroticism, had all passed into the past. Into the most remote past. Don Juan I was growing larger than life. It was an ineffable music of laughter in

17

G-flat, which at times recalled the melodies of Beethoven, of Bach, of Borodin. The laugh concert drew the chorus of oldsters into it, and they too started to laugh uproariously.

Finally, Don Juan I, who was no longer Don Juan I, but the King of Belly Laughs and Guffaws, found the lost chord. At that moment he fell as though struck by lightning. The asinine world-class comedian didn't know what to do. The director had disappeared, and the audience was one rollicking mass of laughter. The light continued to bathe the supine body for several seconds and then switched off. Don Juan I was dying happily and with laughter on his lips. He had outshined Dilurio the Great.

THE MANTLE
OF COMMAND

As soon as he arrived home he took off his new managerial rank and left it lying on the couch. But only for a moment. Almost immediately he picked it up and hung it in the closet. He gazed at it for a bit with mixed emotions—victory, rage, frustration, vengeance—with an undefined emotion, as human emotions often are, and then sat down. He could not help comparing it with the managerial ranks he held at other times, ranks now consigned to oblivion in that closet.

Now his career was really beginning. Now that he had left behind several pasts filled with degrading bootlicking, concealed hatred and administrative envy. Now that his ego had aged and was wrinkled and lacking in strength.

He reflected for a while. At last he was wearing the managerial rank he had always coveted, the rank with which he would be able to make all those wiseguys around him dance to his tune and quake in their boots. It occurred to him that his previous managerial ranks were all like the corpses of an era with no future at the Ministry of Education. He rapidly reviewed all those years of tribulation; he saw himself through a mirror darkly in which he paraded with different ages, holding one rank after the other. Thinking of the new rank—the rank he deserved and which assured him a brilliant future—moved him deeply. The old ranks were there, filed away, exhausted, worn threadbare, patched and tearful. He imagined they were terribly old uniforms he had worn in former times and which had conferred the degrees of importance or non-importance which had been his during the various stages of his life. He saw himself clothed in the wretched rank of Assistant First Class, and later those of Assistant Office Manager, Office Manager, Assistant Supervisor, Supervisor, and now that of Director.

He could not help thinking of Mr. Butt's career, Mr. Butt who was always the great reason for his being passed over. He remembered how each time Butt changed his status, he grew in ego. He pictured him walking, seated, speaking, smoking and even doing strange obscene things, as befitted his disgusting face.

Butt's successive ranks were nothing more than successive abodes for the ego of that case of arrested development, an ego which grew and puffed itself up like a toad. Fortunately, Butt died and now he was the one who was first in line at the door, awaiting his turn to enter. Promotions were like that: there was always someone anxiously waiting on line. Even the candidates for president or dictator or any other position of dignity and glory waited their turn. And they were always on their guard, ready to spring, sharpening their claws like cats, lying in wait like wild beasts, because our animal heritage is never entirely absent. With feelings of repulsion that even the years had not erased, he recalled the occasions on which Mr. Butt ridiculed him and mocked him and denigrated him before his subordinates. He even relived the incident in which Butt called him a filthy, sweating pig in front of Pérez, and once more could see the smirking face of that son-of-a-bitch.

Now it was his turn to enter the upper echelons. The truth is that his guts ached for this promotion, and when Mr. Butt's death was announced he made a very conventional gesture of heartfelt sympathy and shared grief which, in the depths of his being, corresponded to a normal feeling of joy, of animal pleasure. Fleetingly he remembered the prophecy he found himself obliged to fling in Butt's face years before: "You, my dear friend, will soon die, and I will take your place."

The new rank was intangible; it could not be held in the hand. It was like a garment of invisible glass, yet everything changed when he donned it. Those earlier ranks had changed him very little. This latest rank, on the other hand, would give him that big shove that would transform him into a new man.

The rank of Assistant Second Class had done nothing for him. At least he had been very young when he wore it, and he could still wait and wait. All the young men like him could afford to have friends and even to be open and outgoing and not worry about getting ahead, that disease of one's more mature years.

The subsequent promotions had added very little too. Those came during his years of joviality and *joie de vivre*. He told jokes, laughed and engaged in good-humored horseplay. He did everything a young man was supposed to do. It was only when he was promoted to the rank of Office Manager that he felt like a different person. It was then that he discovered he could step on others and squash the loudmouths who had been annoying him. And he would have done just this if it had not been for Mr. Butt who was always present, always ready to countermand him, even though he was under the threat of the prophecy.

He studied himself in the three-way mirror of the bathroom. This mirror provided him with a complete trilateral view. He was partially bald, but this semi-baldness was a sign of strength on every level. He himself was able to feel the strength of the rank. For some time he practiced the stern looks and peevish grimaces he was going to use from then on. He spent several entire evenings on this project. He even tried out new facial expressions: various types of aloofness, of contained fury, of offended dignity, of fierce command, of bluster. And he designed diverse forms of paternalism, of obsequiousness, of disgust, of disdain, of contempt, of condescension. He ended by practicing oratory in the mirror.

"From this moment on I shall live with you. We shall be as one. This is the culmination of my career. You say no, but I say yes. With you I feel strong, powerful. Don't tell me I'm wrong. I'll feel strong and powerful. Mr. Butt is gone. No one will be able to make me crawl. The president, maybe, but the president is a kind of abstraction. You never see him. Now I'll be able to wreak vengeance on all those who stood in the way of my promotion, of my rise to glory. You say I'm too... too vengeful. Nevertheless, it's you who gives me the power to be what I am. Look: now, thanks to you, I'll be able to crush anyone; nobody will snub me now. On the contrary, people will bow and scrape for me. I wonder if it's me or you. Well, we're two in one. You the rank and I the rank holder. And I've almost finished working out the whole package of changes and of forms of conduct that I'm going to put into effect. I've already got my reorganization plans ready. I shall be ruthless."

The managerial rank was all that. It was also the art of speech. The studied roughness of voice, the precise lexeme, the correct moneme, the carefully nuanced tone, feigned indignation. He would be master of the appelative provocation. Without the mantle of command, life would be nothing. What good was the mere body?

"I know that when they see the way I walk, they'll misunderstand me. I won't be able to walk the way I have been. I'm going to have to learn to walk differently. A high-ranking executive's manner of walking is a means of expression. It's a sign, a sign that transmits something, that radiates strength and importance. Everything in life is a sign, and one's manner of walking is a sign of what one is. A high-ranking manager never walks the way he used to in his pre-rank life. He moves deliberately, he looks at people with feigned disdain or with a mask of indifference. Everyone else is just part of the herd, the common crowd. He must free himself of shows of affection and fix the boundaries that will separate him from those who are without high rank. Isn't this true? Yet in certain cases he must possess the indispensable demagogic lucidity to show something that looks like interest, but a cold, conventional, perhaps theatrical, interest. At celebrations I'll arrange for children to kiss me, and I'll pat their little heads the way the Pope does."

The most interesting aspect of his managerial position would be the mental anguish he could inflict, the threat. There was intimidation in the new set of rules and regulations. He no longer had any interest in his friends, not even in Pérez, that great friend of his youth. They were figures from the past. They were history. He would look down on everyone from his superior position. He would be in the monolith. He would be a hierarch and a petrarch. He would be as a stone.

"You tell me I'm wrong again, but I know what I'm saying. I know I must learn, until I know them by heart, a series of masks, and then utilize them. Each mask will be different according to the position within the hierarchy of those I'll be dealing with. Still and all, it will be useful for me to get along well with the maintenance workers and the clerical help. These inferior beings of necessity are always everywhere and can contribute important intelligence reports. It is imperative to maintain an ambiguous relationship with them, a relationship somewhere between paternal and friendly. They know what everyone is doing. They've developed an excellent surveillance system."

Idiots, swine, sons-of-bitches, he would yell at his underlings every day of the week. He would make them crawl.

"Would you mind telling me, you idiot, why you underlined the title of this book instead of putting quotation marks around it?"

"But those are the rules, sir."

"To hell with the rules. Anyway, I'm the one who makes the rules around here. Haven't you ever heard of the chain of command?"

* * *

The title of Director was decisive. It was a far cry from that of Assistant First Class. He didn't even remember that title. It was so insignificant, he didn't even notice it. Back then he could speak with everyone in the same manner. Conviviality, camaraderie, horsing around: these things were a lot of fun, but of no practical value. The position of Director was somewhat difficult. He didn't want to confess it, but he felt as though he were wearing a corset. He could hardly move. But he really felt like an executive. And as time passed and he became hardened, he considered himself more important. After the prophecy, Mr. Butt had not spoken to him any more. He feared him and avoided talking to him out of a superstitious horror. His words resounded in his memory and constituted mental torture: "You will soon die, you'll choke on your own tongue, and I will have your executive rank."

"Yes, soon I'll begin to practice a new way of speaking. I realize I have a few problems with my diction. My English instructor pointed them out to to me. My English instructor…Strange… I need him because we managerial types all have to learn at least some English; it's *de rigueur* at this level. Yet the poor wretch has to be very diplomatic when he corrects me, his superior. But I'll keep at it. I now can say *third* and *fourth* correctly; I don't say *toid* and *fart* any more.

"I'm going to have videos of myself made to correct my way of walking. But what am I going to do with my wife? I don't know how I ever married such an uncultured woman. What's your advice?"

It was very hard for him to relinquish his executive status, to take it off. He no longer did this even in the privacy of his own home. He had always been able to take off his previous ranks easily, even the rank of Office Manager. But not this one. This one had convinced him definitively of his importance. And in his heart of hearts, he felt he could not return to the simplicity of the past. He imagined that this was a managerial rank made to order.

"I shall never be without you now. We will be inseparable. Not even at home will I let you go. Not even in bed or in the bathroom or at meals. You are like those old articles of clothing that one loves so much and mourns for deep inside when they can't be worn any more. Yes, I'll go to the egologist if you think I should."

These days he walked into his house and greeted his family in an artificially formal manner never before seen in him. The family members interpreted this as the result of his being overwhelmed by his work. "The responsibility of his position must be what's making him so introverted and so hard to talk to," his wife thought. The transformation had been gradual. No one noticed at first, but as he donned successive managerial ranks, his personality became progressively more wooden.

His wife remembered him as he had been in the past. He had been jovial and loquacious; especially during the years of their

24

courtship. He had been outgoing, warm and good humored. And, Lord, how sexually aggressive! They went places with friends in those days. It was in the late fifties and the early sixties. They were always doing something and there was plenty of money. Music—the last years of the bolero and the tango—brought out his romantic nature. There were no drugs or violence yet, and the world was better all around. Or so it seemed to her.

"Yes, even in private we'll be together. Only you will know all the secrets of my soul. Neither my wife nor my children will be able to fathom me. Even my aging mother will no longer recognize in me the boy of yesteryear. That boy is still back there in the old neighborhood. He died a long time ago. Now I am an executive; I am all future and no past. You protect and accompany me. Your rod and your staff, they comfort me...

"Just yesterday my wife noticed that I was aloof with her. Well, this is the way it has to be. I'm no longer hers. Not even when we make love. Now there is me and nothing more than me; I am my ego and that is sufficient. I'll confess that with you I feel transformed. Importance, being a VIP, inflames my emotions to such an extent that it turns me into a solitary being. Yes, I understand, I feel more alone than ever. But I am important. You don't say anything. Why? Yesterday I made love. I didn't say one word. I was a robot. I refused to be on intimate terms with my wife."

* * *

Perhaps the successive managerial ranks were having an adverse effect on him. He was becoming wrinkled and frozen of spirit. His facial muscles were losing their tone. His face became inexpressive. It was a process of distancing himself, alienating himself, from everything. The managerial rank received prestigious invitations. Militarily unctuous Germans, painfully polite Frenchmen, unenthusiastically friendly Italians, calculatingly courteous Yankees, etc., etc., came from their embassies with big smiles on their faces and big invitations in their hands. He sat at scores of tables, in scores of cities, with scores of VIP's, one after the other, and repeated scores of managerial-level speeches: *the greatness of the nation; fruit-*

ful negotiations; very productive meeting; positive results...

On certain occasions he experienced an enormous need to feel like an executive. On those occasions, he indulged in truly practical demonstrations of managerial behavior. If he was receiving someone in his office, he adopted certain postures and made use of evasive, aloof language. The language of Administrators. He repeated the terms *specificity, numerical blocks, acculturated* and *misspeak*. He said, for example, "Clearly, the specificity of this function necessitates the utilization of numerical blocks and distinctive emoluments which in turn require acculturated parameters. And they necessitate the elimination of misspeaking, in the presence of the media, that is. If a man misspeaks too often in the presence of the media, this will tend to impact upon his credibility." He then gazed indifferently at his listener, a mere insect so far as he was concerned.

A forgotten rank, the youthful rank of his first position as Assistant, cried out to him from the back of the closet, "What do you want these ranks for, ranks that have more and more power, you old fool? What do you gain with all that new gold braid that will turn you to stone like the Gorgon?"

He was overcome by some sort of uneasiness. Touched by the youthful voice issuing from the closet, he ran to the three-way mirror and stood before it for a long while. His wife was still asleep. He meditated for quite some time. Without his hairpiece, without having shaved, without having massaged his face with the revitalizing ointment, without his false dentures, without the dark glasses that concealed the crow's-feet and the dark circles under his eyes, he felt he was practically a corpse. His low brow gave him the look of an idiot, something the voice from the closet had suggested, and he became extremely depressed. Had his very selfhood, his ego, changed too, he wondered, that ego he loved so. He tried to talk with it, but was unable to make contact. His selfhood or ego was cloaked in the managerial rank, which muffled its voice, preventing it from being heard. Even he could not hear it. There were some who maintained that the self or the ego was imperishable, that it was not ruled by the laws of the material world. He would have liked to compare his present ego with that of yesteryear. He felt the same as ever. He liked young women, young people, everything in the world that was spring-like. He was the same being he had been before. But whoever looked at his face and observed his slow pace saw a dilapidated ego. He heard another cry from the youthful managerial rank in the closet: "Wouldn't you like to be with me, to go out with me the way we used to, you old fool, fool of an ego, even if you had to be on a first-name basis with everyone and wallow with ordinary people, with young people?" He thought about his ego being wrinkled and battered, about its being an aged ego without strength or courage. He promised himself he would go to the egologist. That's what he was an executive for. That's what he had money for. The egologist would set his odometer back to zero.

* * *

His wife is worried. She doesn't understand what is happening. He never takes off his new managerial rank. He eats with his rank on, he sleeps with his rank on, performs all his bodily functions with his rank on. He even thinks with his rank on. Maybe he'll die with his rank on.

"I'll tell you the truth: you're useful to me. You're going to allow me to accomplish great things, like becoming rich, for example. You are power, opportunity, decision-making capacity. And all that will be inside me. It will take up residence in me for a time, and I will be happy, very happy. Later, when you abandon me, it won't matter any more. My ego will have been long gone and forgotten. It will be nothing but a little piece of history or a little piece of the great void. Who will care about what I've done! What difference does it make what a man does! People judge everything in life the way they want to judge it. Good is bad and bad is good. What no one can take away from us is material pleasure, the pleasures of this world. Who cares if I trample on the less fortunate! With the passage of time even murderers are no longer murderers. Just a couple of years are enough. Everything changes, new people come along, those who were here earlier disappear, one establishment is followed by another and another and still another. No one will remember me, clothed in you. Some old man with a long memory will mention something about me, anywhere at all; everyone will laugh and go on to the next matter. Whatever is

27

new and throbbing with life always triumphs over the past. Each minute sets a gravestone over the preceding minute. The great mistake is to flagellate ourselves for our actions. I think only of myself and of the moment in which I'm living. I'm speaking frankly to you. You are my strength, my open sesame. To hell with what other people think, with the judgement of history. History is nothing but a filing cabinet, facts in mothballs, a form of petrification of interest only to specialists. What is mine—my advantages in life, my possessions, my triumphs, my enjoyment at anyone's expense—will be something that no one will remember."

He feels his importance is so great that he cannot take off his executive rank even to take a bath. Or rather, he feels that if he does take it off, he will cease to be important. He senses that men in themselves are nothing. Rank is everything. He thinks about what Mr. X was with his rank and what he was without it. As soon as one dons a managerial rank, he ceases to be what he is. People treat him differently. "And what do you think, Mr. López, sir?" "And you, Mr. General Manager, sir, Mr. President, sir, could you evaluate...?" the newspapermen ask with an interest that is automatic. And if he's a soccer player: "And what does the great Rodriguez think of the Spanish soccer team?" Those who have no rank hover around those who have it. They try to hang around them, get close to them. If at a cocktail party there is a high-ranking executive standing at point X, the plebeian or semi-plebeian begins by sidling up to the executive. He or she distractedly attempts to grasp a sandwich or a cold-cut that happens to be near the rank holder. Then he or she stands right next to him. The rank holder speaks with other rank holders, but suddenly, when he tries to pick up a sandwich, their hands make contact. It is at this point that the desired communication is established.

"Aren't these sandwiches"—or cakes, or candies, or whatever—"delicious!" And at times a conversation develops.

He hardly speaks at the office. He utilizes monosyllables a great deal. He converses about something with his fellow executive, Mr. P., but only a few words. He thinks a great deal. He doesn't trust his fellow executive.

"I know that you are a kind of entelechy, that materially you

28

are a zero, that an overcoat has more existence than you. Nevertheless, what power you have over a person! What a capacity for transformation! How have you done this? How did you take that petty individual who used to live hunched over a desk and turn him into this great and powerful being that I am now? What do I care about the plans for the future of the country and of the department! It is my selfhood, my ego that I'm interested in. I'm only interested in myself, nothing else.

At last he had his appointment. The visit to the egologist was outrageous! He arose that day feeling very nervous. He had to remove his managerial rank. He did this in the bathroom, where no one could see him. Without it he felt like a wretched specimen. He didn't know what to do with himself.

The egologist's receptionist had him go in. She hardly took notice of him; for her, the executive was simply a broken-down, trembling old man.

The egologist didn't see him, nor did he see the egologist. At least that was his impression. He was aware only of a face on a video screen, a voice asking him questions, and nothing else. It was an electronic or cybernetic visit. The egologist spoke in atonal syllables:

> make-your-self-com-fort-able-I-want-to-see-
> your-e-go-slide o-ver-to-your-left-bend-o-ver-
> I-want-to-see-the-fool-ish-and-vis-cous-
> parts-of-your-e-go-do-not-move

He sat before the screen for fifteen minutes, trembling and crying at times like an aged child. He had to sit at a table, eat chicken and French-fried potatoes, then carry out various bodily functions and finally make love with a robot of infinite mechanical beauty from the Isles of Nippon. He was photographed and photometered in every phase of these tests. At one point he moaned and began to say, "Doctor, tell me, please..."

The egologist's face in black and white returned to the screen, expressionless, inscrutable. Then said, "Examination terminated. You may pick up the results on March second at 11:50 A.M."

The screen dimmed and the face disappeared.

He now takes twenty-two different kinds of pills. He continues to understand that his new managerial rank allows him no time to be expansive. He doesn't speak at all. A time will come when he will be admitted to a hospital somewhere with some problem or other. There he'll be with his managerial rank securely donned. His ego, his selfhood, will be nothing but his rank. The doctors will make some diagnosis or other. Perhaps he'll be buried with his managerial rank. Perhaps he'll continue to be an executive. Perhaps he'll go sailing around heaven cloaked in his managerial rank and won't even say hello to the Lord. Perhaps.

THE LETTER

Buenos Aires, August 5, 1983

Miss Iwona Andersson
Sveagatan, 20
123 11 Goteborg
Sweden

Dear Iwona:

  I have decided to straighten my things out a bit today. I've made up my mind to throw out a lot of papers, the kind of papers that accumulate on my desk and in the closet without my even noticing it. I'm not the sort of person who likes to throw anything out, but sometimes I have to do it. All my papers, my plane tickets, and even some receipts from stores in which I once bought something or other, are sacred to me. They're like relics. They bring me back to the past; in a way they kind of make time stand still. Or more than that: they eternalize the past which keeps slipping through our fingers. I once considered putting all my papers into a folder and keeping them there the way entomologists mount insects on pins so they can come back to them and look at them from time to time, but I haven't progressed beyond the thinking stage. I would like to see my tickets and my scraps of paper pasted firmly in an album: Hotel Ost, Augsburg DM.50, Tunnelbanan, Vinter-tabell 1978, Luchtpost, Hauptbahnhoff, Londonkollegiet.

Most people return from a trip and throw everything out. And forget about everything. I don't throw anything out. That's why the cleaning lady sometimes complains to me. She asks me how I can live among so many scraps of paper faded by time, among so many old, worn objects. I enjoy these things of mine. The little scraps of paper, the notes, the tickets and even the little match boxes and cigarette packs brought back from my trips recreate in my mind situations which perhaps were unimportant at the time but which now takes on gigantic proportions because they reconstruct the past. A chit for currency exchange in Istanbul, for example, triggers dozens of experiences in my mind. I'm back in the Great Bazaar; I'm crossing the Golden Horn on a ferry, I see myself once more in a café on Galata Street or on Taksim Square. A receipt for the purchase of a necktie brings me back to Warsaw; a card kept as a souvenir places me in Bucharest once more. Then I relive things, relive them intense-ly. I relive a moment that was unique in the history of my mind.

Routine, odious routine, is nothing more than the reiteration of absolutely the same situation until it becomes a sort of chain of events in which there are practically no differences: A once; A twice; A thrice. Office workers suffer from a kind of malady because of this—because they repeat the same thing day after day. Seven a.m.: take a shower; seven-thirty: have breakfast; eight o'clock: leave the house; nine: at the office. Then the hours roll by. The wall, the desk, the insipid remark, the coffee break and, finally, out the door. Nothing special. Your mind contracts, becomes devitalized and ends by becoming closed to everything. As the years go by, habit becomes so strong that any kind of change is a tragedy. Not being able to have your tea at four o'clock is a kind of cataclysm for *homo rutinarius*.

It must strike you as odd that someone you don't know, who does not yet click in your mind, would begin a letter in this way. Just a few days ago I found the plane ticket to and from your city. And in one corner of the ticket, your name and address.

Ten whole years have passed, and I'm wondering if these lines will make their way to your nerve centers. And if you will remember me.

I remember snatches of our relationship as one recalls a melody. I can still see you seated on the Polish airplane. I can even feel how cold it was on the runway. And how cold it was in the plane flying at ten thousand feet with no heat. And the Poles, square-shouldered and stuffed into their thick, dark overcoats.

What a strange world it is! People make new acquaintances thousands of feet in the air. Nothing has ever come of it in my case, but I know of others whose entire lives have been changed by these encounters.

You could have changed the course of my life. Maybe I wasn't decisive enough. That's why I go on the same as always. The same as always and in my fifties. You came into my mind, which is my life, suddenly, and went out of it almost immediately. Everything in life is fortuitous. It could have been some other person who came into my life. It could have been some overweight gentleman, a priest, an elderly lady. You could have taken some other seat on the plane, and I wouldn't have known anything about your life. I might have met so many other people!

I thought a great deal about what you said to me on that trip. I thought about it for several days. Later, as always happens, time erased the images. I was all wrapped up in myself, deep in thought, for several days. I checked into a hotel in Hamburg, on G. Strasse, and tried to do something. There was still a chance. Besides, a Polish woman was something special, something grand, in my estimation. She was different from a German woman or a French woman or an Italian woman.

The thought of you, thirty years old, married to an elderly Swedish gentleman, a seventy-five year old man, gnawed at me for a long time. Especially all the time I was in Hamburg. I realize the man had done it for your benefit. That he asked nothing of you. That he had done it out of humanity alone, so that you could remain in Sweden, so you could work, succeed in your career as a ballerina. But…well…I saw you bound to another human being, to a man. I was what might be called jealous. What a strange world it is. Someone you couldn't even have imagined being jealous, and he is jealous ten years later.

We were flying over the Baltic when you told me all that. A stewardess brought us coffee. Coffee and a piece of cake. The coffee was terrible, the cake was stale, and the cold was atrocious. But still and all, there was a wonderful enchantment to our conversation. The enchantment a man always feels when he's with a woman who is attractive and at the same time sorrowful, vulnerable, possibly not well-treated by life. Perhaps these mini-romantic situations that occur in today's world are the motivating force of our lives. Surrounded by so many machines, human contact might be a sort of light in the gloom, a window on life. I can tell you that since I found the ticket and your name, I have been very happy. I rush home from my daily routine, and I speak with you. Up until a little while ago, when you lay neglected in my memory, I didn't know what to do with myself. At times I even uttered insults and obscenities to myself. Now I'm back on board the Lot airliner, at an altitude of ten thousand feet over the Baltic, chattering away. I'm genuinely happy.

I'm wondering what ever happened to you. That's why I'm writing. And I'm sure you will answer me. I still retain in my memory the first words we spoke to each other at the Warsaw airport. I had been sightseeing in your city the day before. It was winter. I received the impression of a city in which people lived in hiding. In hiding within their own souls. The people were like that enormous black Palace of Science and Culture, like that immense dark phantom located at the center of the city, which at nightfall blended with the shadows and at dawn began to take on its own outlines. And you too, dressed in black, had emerged from that world. Strangely enough, everyone seemed suffused with the joy of living. And there was an eagerness to be helpful. I still remember you in your black overcoat; there was something bohemian, defeated, dispirited, about you. You had not yet attained the importance or the impudence conferred by fine new clothes. You even had about you the smell of those not favored by fortune. You were not subject to the consumer society and were untouched by artificial odors.

Maybe you had emerged from one of those ancient houses.

Perhaps from some dwelling on the other side of the Vistula, that old river called the Vistula. Perhaps from some squalid little apartment in the Prague quarter, that quarter which was like a relic and which impressed me so much. Perhaps you had risen from the grey waters, from the thick Vistula fog, from some Polish poem. Perhaps you were the daughter of one of those wintry ladies wearing babushkas and hawking their wares at the Prague Street market.

I can still see you with the little bottle of vodka you bought before take-off: Zytnia Extra Vodka. I associate you with Warsaw all the time. I associate you with the streets, with the buildings, even with the greyishly warm climate of your country. Because I have always thought that behind the greys there is a great human warmth, and that behind the brazenness of the brilliant, scorching sun, the shameless sunlight of the Mediterranean, is only coldness. But all this is subjective.

My nocturnal strolls along Marszalkowska, along the Alleja Jerosolimska and along Spitalna and Rudkiego are linked in my mind with you, and I wonder about your avatars. Last night I felt myself walking those streets and I could see myself prying, snooping, into those apartment buildings, and I thought that you must be in one of them, drinking tea, *herbatá*, as the stewardess called it. I really saw myself as though in a motion picture. Have you ever seen yourself walking, stopping for a moment, looking at something? I have. I've even imagined I was two people. The one on the outside and the one on the inside. The one on the outside with an indomitable life of his own. The inner one, pensive and indecisive.

I've spent about two hours staring at a picture I once bought of the city of Warsaw. I've pictured the plane landing in Copenhagen. They were the last moments of our brief relationship. Well, at least it occurred to me to ask you to have a cup of coffee with me at the airport. It's a pity it was only for a few brief minutes. I would have liked to tell you something, something more beautiful, more intimate, from the depths of my being to your being, but I don't know if you were aware of my need. Maybe the different atmosphere of Denmark, the machine-like airport employees, broke the spell. Because for everything that really counts in life one must go beyond mere reality.

Perhaps, had I been bolder, the course of our lives might have been changed. Perhaps I wouldn't have stood staring pensively at a picture for an hour today.

Maybe all these things I'm telling you sound cloying, mawkish, as though I'm whining. You'll have to make a real effort to remember that you were once with a fellow passenger having coffee in Copenhagen. Sometimes one expects too much from others. One hopes they will remember him, that they will have him fixed in their memories. Nonsense.

Still, I hope that in spite of everything, these lines, which are no longer just a few lines, find their way into your hands. Or, rather, into your life. The truth is that I myself have been a friend, a very faithful friend of yours, from the time we clasped hands at the airport.

Now I've been thinking we ought to get together again. I don't want to wait for this to happen in another life in which everything will happen all over again just as it did ten years ago. We'll walk together once more, not holding hands as they do in romantic stories, but like two ordinary people. We won't be together on some hurried journey, at an altitude of ten thousand feet, on a cold, viewless flight. The streets of Warsaw or of any city at all will be more hospitable, less cosmic, less sidereal.

I really long to see you. Forgive me for telling you how I feel. Your straight black hair, your dark eyes, your long, slender hands, have not been erased from my mind. I'd be grateful just to take a walk with you one afternoon. It would be nice if it were in Warsaw.

And now I shall be waiting for your letter. I am sure that I shall soon be watching desperately for the mailman. I'll stand at the window and look out.

Cordially, your friend,
Juan González

MR. SZOMOGY'S
BEST FRIEND

Mr. Szomogy came to the consulate one summer morning. The switchboard operator called me on the intercom and told me there was an individual there who wanted some information; she even gave me his name. The man was rather tall, actually just plain tall, and bore some resemblance to a camel. I couldn't say why I immediately made a mental connection between Szomogy and a camel. Maybe it was the expression on his very Central European face.

"What can I do for you?" I inquired in the usual courteous tone of voice I used with everyone.

"Look here. I have come to the consulate because I confess a great admiration for your country," he explained with an accent I detected to be Hungarian. "Yes, I confess a really great enthusiasm."

Mr. Szomogy made a lateral movement with one of his legs, reminding me of a dromedary. When we shook hands he bowed and attempted a toothy smile which he did not complete, perhaps because of timidity. He bowed his head with an automatic and well trained humility, and a sort of hump formed on the site of his first vertebra. It seemed to me that his eyes were devoid of life or expression, that they were something like the eyes of a statue, or that they revealed some kind of abnormality.

"How can I help you, Mr. Szomogy?" I said, smoothly diving into that sea of strange anxieties and courageous smiles and of teeth covered with the tartar of years of neglect, into that sea of blank stares, of humps and uncoordinated sidestepping. The man said nothing. His mind seemed to be elsewhere for several seconds as he just stared at me. At last he said, "I would like to know something about your country. I know they have a great system of social welfare and a great sense of friendship."

I asked him to wait a few moments, and I returned to the reception room with the latest brochures. The switchboard operator stared at the ceiling in boredom. Mr. Szomogy had seated himself on a comfortable modern sofa and seemed to experience some moments of insulated happiness in which, judging by his face, he thought of nothing. When I brought it to his attention that I was ready to hand him the brochures, he sprang to his feet and bowed, forming an angle of thirty or forty degrees with his torso and head.

I was very busy and so found some way to put an end to the interview. I extended my hand and informed him that I was at his service. In spite of the handicap of his emaciated physique and his age, Mr. Szomogy came to attention like a European soldier, thanked me and bowed once more, this time at a vigorous angle of sixty degrees.

Out of the corner of my eye I tried to make something of his facial expression, but it seemed to me to be inscrutable or perhaps stupid; at times I couldn't distinguish between the two. Altogether, tearful feelings aside, there was a certain something about him that made me think he might be a wretchedly unhappy man, that his soul would crumple whenever he tried to speak, that he was trying to overcome some sort of impediment, but was not succeeding because he didn't have the strength, the skill, the cunning, the power. He seemed to lack the ability for pretense in his dealings with others, that minimum dose of affectation and hypocrisy so necessary in life for attracting and snaring human beings. He gave the impression of pinning all his hopes on correct behavior, on a rigid mechanical correctness, on courteous, even genuflective, manners, which in his mind were interpreted as the ideal behavior and the key to success. It was obvious that he had never thought of the weapon of charm, of elegance, of deceit, of the well-prepared lie, or of subtle, genial adulation. He could not manage to go beyond the rigid confines of a repetitious and single-minded correctness, the heritage, perhaps, of a feudal past of boyar torturers and conquering Attilas.

When he returned one month later, I was genuinely surprised. I hadn't thought he would come back. He spoke to me about the brochures, about the cities and even about the standard of living of the country we represented. The Consul, a ruddy-cheeked fellow with the eyes of a wild boar, happened to be passing through the reception room as I was speaking with him. Later he called me in and said, "There's no need to waste time with those weirdos. This country is teeming with these annoying pains-in-the-ass who have nothing better to do than to come to the Consulate looking for folders and brochures. What we're interested in here is business, import permits, export permits, in other words, money."

I went back to my desk without a word. This time the brief conversation with Mr. Szomogy had been truncated because I received a long-distance call. Even so, I remember his more than sixty-degree bow and the clammy hand he extended as he left, and I remember the enormous head, the inexpressive face and then the long back and the dark hat leaving by the front door.

The janitor informed me that Mr. Szomogy had stopped by once more during my vacation.

Almost at the end of the year the switchboard operator called me on the intercom to say there was a gentleman to see me in the reception room. Szomogy was waiting for me once more. He looked more emaciated. Maybe more inexpressive. Strangely inexpressive, with an inexpressivity that was paradoxically quite expressive, and that I later tried to understand. His grey suit was more threadbare than ever, as were his shirt and tie, but one could see that he was making an effort to maintain his decorum, the pathetic decorum of those who refuse to succumb to poverty. If suits and shirts and ties and shoes were able to speak, Mr. Szomogy's clothing would have cried to heaven that they were dying, that they were disintegrating, that they could not bear it any longer on that long, bony body which didn't harbor the slightest idea of how to survive. Even the idea of stealing something would never occur to him. His entire plan for survival hinged on one course of action: correctness, meekness. Szomogy no longer even spoke. He emitted a very offensive odor, a fetid odor, the smell of decay. The only thing he did was to extend his hand to me, a hand that was like a pile of large bones around which my own hand could hardly close. It occurred to me that if I had been able to squeeze it, the phalanges, the carpus and the metacarpus would break or fly into pieces, and that I would be left with one of the digital bones or the trapezoid in my fist.

In spite of everything, among those bones covered with a strangely damp and wrinkled skin, there was still a touch of human warmth, a warmth that seemed to be begging for contact, communication, friendship. And that was what constituted the expressiveness of the inexpressivity. It was that enormous skeleton which, with the burden of his declining years, attained a fifty-degree bow only with enormous effort.

For several moments I didn't know what to do. He didn't say a word. He stood there with his dark fedora in his hand, staring as though he were expecting something to happen, expecting some event to take place. I asked him, as I had on the two previous occasions, if he wanted anything. "No, sir," he answered with an almost cavernous voice and an accent that was more foreign than ever. I didn't know what to do to break the ice, or the siege, or whatever it was that he unintentionally was subjecting me to. The worst thing about it was that I felt as though I were paralyzed. There I was, facing Szomogy. I was looking at him, and he was looking at me, and the time was passing. Fortunately, the switchboard operator had gone out for a few minutes, and there was no one there to observe what undoubtedly must have been a strange scene. Two men standing, facing one another, not a word being spoken. Had the Consul—a man who outdid himself to be amiable and unctuously courteous when he sensed an advantage to be gained—passed by at that moment, he would have raked me over the

40

coals. Maybe he would have fired me for wasting my time on some poor devil. It occurred to me that maybe I could help Mr. Szomogy in some way. I didn't know how. I had no idea. Or rather, I had an idea, although it was somewhat fuzzy. Maybe at night he slept in one of those shanties made of tarpaper and refuse that scavengers set up in vacant lots; maybe he managed in one of those ruined buildings in the old city, in which rats, or men already passed into their decline, take shelter, maybe... who knows what.

Very slowly I slipped my hand into my trousers pocket, took out ten pesos and carefully extended my hand as though to say goodbye, and slipped them into something that was no longer a palm. "No thank you, sir," was all he said. I thought I perceived a fleeting flicker of gratitude in his eyes, those eyes that had something Asiatic about them.

Two weeks later a dark-complected woman came to the Consulate and asked to speak to me. She explained that Mr. Szomogy had passed away. A few days before he had asked her very insistently to come and thank me. He told her that I was a good friend of his, actually his best friend, and that if something were to happen to him he wished that someone would transmit his sense of deepest gratitude to me. The woman told me that Szomogy had been found dead precisely in one of those ruined buildings, and that she had known him for years, but had spoken with him very rarely. That was why it had struck her as odd that Szomogy had asked this favor of her. Szomogy's corpse, stretched out on the floor, swollen and in a state of decomposition, had been found by some boys. They had hit a ball into the ruined building, which was a lucky thing because in that way they discovered Szomogy and prevented the body from decomposing even further.

The dark lady also told me where he had been buried, and one afternoon of that same month of May I went to the cemetery. The sun shone brightly and the birds warbled in the tops of the cypress trees. I couldn't locate the spot in which she had told me Mr. Szomogy lay buried, but I supposed he was right around there somewhere, and I took a moment of remembrance for him. I could think freely there because there was no chance of the Consul's showing up. I remembered Szomogy's mild but motionless eyes and his hands. The organs which best express a man's inner being, that is.

The dark lady had told me that his grey suit had become rags, that his undershirt and his shoes were coming apart, and that she had seen him like that, in that condition, trying for the last time to make his way along a street near the waterfront, perhaps trying to find a scrap of food. His hat was the article of clothing which had fared best. Now the dark lady's husband—he too had a large head—was wearing it. It came in handy for him on rainy days when he poked among the rubbish of the downtown stores in search of scraps of paper.

Biographical or Bio-statistical note:

F. Szomogy was born of the union of Maria Szabo and Janos Szomogy, on 1-22-15 as a result of the act of sexual intercourse number 372 of this married couple in the little city of Kaposvar in the southern part of the country. It was a lovely spring evening. Maria and Janos, who were on vacation, had taken a stroll through a nearby little wood, felt happy, romantic, overflowing with the life force, and had made love. The spermatazoon which engendered Szomogy penetrated Maria's ovule one split-second before its nearest neighbor could. Had that other one penetrated first, Mr. Szomogy might never have developed such a close friendship with the man at the consulate.

THE LOSER

For a whole mess of years, Catalino, some other guys from the bank and I would get together every Friday night at Facal's Bar, chewing the fat till all hours of the night about anything at all. When the building—actually, a mansion from the late 1890s—was demolished, we switched to a different place. We took our business to a joint on Sierra Street, that venerable old Sierra Street that had just been renovated with a new cement job. When Mr. Fernández Crespo showed up with a more modern touch of distinction, the street had to resign itself and change, not its location as we did, but by taking the new name of Fernández Crespo Street.

So, with all these new things, the old, peeling walls of this little café and the racket made by the loudmouths who always turned up at about eleven o'clock at night and sat down in the back, we kept up our Friday chit-chats. I always wondered—and so did Catalino—how it was that we ended up in that decrepit old café. The truth is that the things the old gang used to do were a mystery. There was always someone who gave an order, as happens in the governing body of a political party, and

43

the whole group would move as a unit. Whoever wouldn't go along with it was branded a disloyal friend, or a non-conformist or just a wise-assed son-of-a-bitch, so everyone kept his mouth shut and went along with the gang. But we never knew where the idea of doing this, that, or the other thing came from: to go to some bungalow on the beach at Solymar one Sunday, on another to a farm house at Las Piedras, to organize a barbecue on one occasion and a ravioli dinner on another, and so on and so forth.

Sierra Street, or Fernández Crespo Street, or whatever you want to call it, was a very special street, and in a way it was worth it to get out of the downtown area. It had a sort of soul to it, a sort of life of its own—actually, every street has a soul and life of its own—the soul and life that people always instill in the things they frequent, especially if they aren't dominated by the denaturalizing effects of snobbery, the way the downtown yuppies are.

On our new—but actually old—street there were some very small and indeterminate stores, relics from the pre-paved days when it was called Sierra Street, which gave it the look of a Turkish bazaar. A little after nightfall, a weak little yellowish light was turned on in each one of them, a light you noticed because of the purest, strictest sense of thrift it indicated. The planet would endure for a long time with men like these, because they were very frugal in the use they made of energy resources.

Catalino and Gabriel felt the magnetic exoticism of Sierra Street, too, and they even talked about those shops. In one of them—I remember this very clearly—there shone a dirty and almost pitiful bulb that scarcely illuminated the bald head of an ageless man who manipulated some indeterminate tool in the mysterious back room—a man perhaps like other men, who probably ate, cohabitated, and even defecated from time to time. In another shop an old lantern, suspended from a ceiling covered with cobwebs, shed hardly any light on a man with a sallow olive complexion, a black moustache, and a flat head, maybe an Armenian shoemaker, who muttered words in Turkish and furiously hammered on shoe soles placed on an iron last.

On the corner of a side street with almost no street lights, somewhat removed from the downtown zone where Sierra Street crosses Miguelete, a very short little man, who gave me the impression of being a Spaniard, always moved about among barrels of *maté yerba* tea leaves, sacks most likely of potatoes, and worn wooden cases that had lost their original color. Sometimes I stopped near the store and inhaled—in a state of ecstasy—that aroma which was a blend of hundreds of things—Spanish sardines, sausages, cheeses, intermingled with kerosene, spices, oils—some of them in a pre-fermented state, others already undergoing fermentation. The ineffable combination of the store's contents was intoxicating. It was the most sublime poetry, the poetry of the sense of smell, so neglected by the bards, who instead lived in the exultant sweetness of majestic opulence and never noticed these micro-worlds. When I would finally arrive at the café, I'd be unable to speak with the boys for quite a few minutes, because I was still under the spell of that potpourri or aromas. Sometimes I came on foot from downtown, and would stop on the bridge and peer down. Everything was blackish. Only a puddle would reflect any light.

In a fish store that disappeared a short time later and which was always in a kind of semi-twilight, I often heard a ruddy-faced elderly woman mumble strange things with a very strong Italian accent. The fishy odor, both disgusting and appetizing at the same time, transported me to the sea, and I felt as though I were on a sailing ship, anxiously inhaling the salt air. I was enthralled by the shellfish, the hake, cod, porgies, all the undersea fauna. And Friday after Friday, I stopped at that store to glory in it all with passion. Sometimes I stopped in front of the store and inhaled with pleasure, lowering my head so people couldn't tell what I was doing. At those times I got the feeling that I was in some exotic city, on a dream-like Istiklal Street in Istanbul, about which I had heard so much from Pepe Conforte, my deceased Sephardic Jewish friend from Turkey.

* * *

The boys would talk about anything at all. Sometimes they

even reached the point of shouting. Paroli didn't go only on Fridays; he went every single night. At nine o'clock he'd have his foot on the rail and converse with anyone who was within range. The point was to say something, to communicate. If no one was around, he talked to the Spaniard who owned the place and that was that. He wasn't selective. Anyone at all suited him. And slowly but surely he'd finish off a drink, and then another one, and then still another, and then at midnight he'd have one for the road. Sometimes, if something unforeseen came up, he downed another shot and then another and another again until he got pretty well loaded. And then he talked and even talk-talk-talked your ear off until they closed up and pushed him out the door. He never ran out of steam.

* * *

I always wondered what was in the back room, in the murky gloom of the storeroom of this café. The Spaniard went back there and then returned every once in a while. There was a great darkness back there; it was like the den of some large animal. But the Spaniard went back there, was submerged in the darkness, and always returned with something: with a bottle, a cheese, a pork sausage, anything at all.

He was an inexpressive man. Physically, he was very different from a Japanese person, but fundamentally just as inscrutable. No one knew what he was thinking or what his goals were in that world of alcoholic fumes, habitual semi-drunks—for whom he had a high tolerance—never attempting to contradict... What strange psyches they had, those men like him from ancient towns like Pontevedra or La Coruña or Orense in Northwestern Spain!

Catalino still felt "homesick" for the downtown landscape and commented that he missed seeing all those people who walked along the main drag, that he missed the large front window at Facal's and the dark brown wooden chairs and little tables that for him were like friends, girl friends, I believe, and the white demitasse cups and the little lumps of sugar. And he complained that now he was served his coffee in a glass—an act of treason to the palate—and that the sugar came in a sort of closed glass that ended in a tube you had to turn upside down, and the granulated sugar came out in dribs and drabs because it was always moist.

* * *

Catalino's love life was totally unknown to us. He never spoke—the way other men do, like Risso the Stud, for example—about his conquests. He *did* tell jokes about women and even dirty jokes (every once in a while he repeated the story of the constipated dwarf), but he had never been seen mixed up with skirts. You always wondered if he had ever had a sexual experience or simply had ever been in love, and even about how there could be men like that, without any sex life or love life. There was this Díaz fellow, a boy who came to the café a couple of times and later died of peritonitis, who once mentioned that he had seen Catalino go into a whorehouse on Río Branco Street, in a big hurry and sort of nervously sneaky-like, with a large briefcase, but we could get no further information on this. Maybe that was the whole of Catalino's sexual universe, a universe that lasted eight or ten minutes and provided him with material for the repertoire from which he later extracted dirty jokes as though he were a great connoisseur.

So, the crush he got on fat María Teresa—230 pounds, 43 years old—or the hots he had for her, or however you want to put it, was something incredible and entirely unforeseen. We never found out how or where they met. Ibarra the Basque came in once with the story that they had met at a wake and that after the interment of the remains of so-an-so in the vault of the Buceo Cemetery, she took him in her Fiat Topolino to the offices of the Internal Revenue Service and that they agreed to see each other one Friday in '72—during the time of President Bordaberry—when he didn't show up at the café. But this was nothing more than a rumor, because the truth was that he continued to show up for a while after this.

* * *

Catalino never said a word about his love life, and in the café he never spoke of anything but the office until one week before getting married. You could just tell that he couldn't get away from that magnet formed by the four bare walls among which he spent his days. You could see that the files, the dossiers, the notes and the papers were permanently at the center of his consciousness, and that without them he was uncomfortable. Just as soon as possible, he'd get into administrative matters and laws and inheritance matters and situations that he repeated *ad infinitum* and which gushed as though from a fountain, inundating his mind and making him rejoice in the strange pleasure that routine has always imposed on humankind.

One day, a Friday as usual, he got there as though he were part of an accelerated motion picture. He was in a highly excited state and talking non-stop about an old woman who had left her estate, consisting of several houses and apartments in the comfortable Pocitos district and in the high-rent zone downtown, to a Spaniard who owned a department store and who, they said, had been her lover. She hadn't remembered her sisters, who lived miserably on a wretched pension and cried their eyes out over it all night long at the Sunset Funeral Home. "It can't be, it can't be," they shouted. "He didn't even have the decency to come to the wake for ten minutes, that animal of a Spaniard, but he sure knew how to pocket the cash in a hurry."

* * *

After the wedding, Catalino came only one time to have coffee with us. We still wonder how that could have been. It was exactly a month after he got married. It was a Friday in May. He took a seat without saying a word, took the glass of coffee and dropped a Sucaryl tablet into it. He explained that sugar, according to *her*—he didn't refer to her Christian name—is bad for you, and then never opened his mouth again for the rest of the evening. He didn't tell even one of those dirty jokes he always used to come prepared with. After a while he glanced at his pocket watch and said, "Well, gentlemen, yours truly will be on his way." And that was it. He left. Good old Catalino in his familiar dark overcoat went out by the front door and disappeared into the night.

Months went by and he never came back. He didn't come even once to have a cup of coffee and be with the old gang for so much as ten minutes. When Gabriel called him at the office, they told him that Catalino couldn't come to the phone. He called three times, but it was always the same story. And when he went to wait for him at the entrance to the bank, he saw Fatty there waiting and didn't have the nerve to do anything. He just stood there for a while thinking, saw him leave slowly, walk toward her, meekly let her take his arm and cross the street, and get into the Fiat Topolino, squeezed up real tight against Fatty.

When I called him at home, she answered the phone. This happened two, three, four times. And when I said I wanted to talk to him, there was always some excuse. Either he was in the bathroom, or in bed, or he had laryngitis or a toothache or anything at all, but Catalino never came to the phone. He was totally out of circulation.

We always figured that some day he would unexpectedly turn up at the café and that everything would return to normal, but it was obvious that the Doctrine of Cycles or of the Eternal Return refused to go into effect. Her lord and master, Catalino López Marchetti, was under lock and key and was not about to appear.

I once saw them coming up the main drag downtown. They were walking toward me arm in arm. As usual he was held fast by Fatty's arm and looked as though he were a prisoner. They gave the impression of being wrapped up in their own affairs and of not seeing anything around them. An idea came to me right on the spot. I got up my courage and stepped in front of them.

"Hello there, good people," I said.

There was no response.

"This guy has his nerve. He wants to hit us up for a loan," Fatty said and dragged him off with all the strength of her 230 pounds. They disappeared in the crowd, and there I was with egg on my face. But I'd managed to see Catalino's wife close up, and then I spent several days trying to apply my knowledge of phrenology. She was a large robust creature. She almost appeared to be a man, and, I might add, one of the stronger types of men. She even had a man's voice, and, what's more, she seemed meticulously shaved, as though she wanted to conceal her hormonal problem. Her domineering, almost dictatorial, personality could be seen shining right through her ruddy complexion.

49

Rather than discouraging me, this spurred me on further. It put me in a bad mood, and I decided to attempt something more elaborate. I had several different ideas: Show up at their house unexpectedly; go to his office; phone him once more; send a telegram. I had to find a way to get Catalino out of his new surroundings and speak with him. Somebody had to help him, I kept telling myself.

I called the house once more, and she answered again. Well, *she* was always the one who picked up the phone, the fat bitch, because *he* was always taking a bath. He must have been the cleanest man in the world. Anyway, I asked for Catalino and told her that all his friends wanted to see him, etc., etc. Her answer was that he still had a lot to learn, and she said something about old aunts, and about old cronies, and this, that and the other thing. And that he was a jerk because sometimes, when it was very cold, he would go off to visit an old aunt of his out in La Teja, leaving Fatty alone for a few hours.

"The guy's a loser, and I'm going to have to teach him a thing or two," she practically shouted.

"Yes, I understand," I said.

"He goes off and spends hours and hours with his aunt, with this aunt who can't even hear or see anymore. She's a worn-out old dish rag with hardened arteries, and he leaves me here in the apartment, all by myself, with nothing to do, because, as you can imagine, I can't stand those old Gardel tangoes or any of that whole collection of tango records he has."

"Then why don't you go with him to see his aunt?" it occurred to me to ask.

"Who, me? Go see that ridiculous woman, that piece of garbage who, just because she raised him, thinks she owns him?"

There was some noise on the telephone line, the kind of static you get every day, a couple of *hello hello*es, and we picked up the conversation once more.

"Stay in the bathtub, you animal!" I heard her shouting.

"Hello, hello," I repeated.

"Excuse me, I was speaking to Catalino. I have to be very strict with him, because he's just like a child," she said.

The conversation didn't last much longer.

It occurred to me the next day that the best way to get in

touch with him again was to make friends with one of the officials at the bank. I knew Miguelito Palombo very well, and by coincidence I ran into him one afternoon downtown. Maybe it wasn't so much of a coincidence after all, since I always used to hang around the main drag, near the family. He had this great big bag of cookies, and among them you could see some chocolate ones, which he'd liked since he was a little kid because they were nice and crunchy and fresh. It was cold outside, so we went into the Paponia Café.

I really enjoyed strolling along the main drag, seeing the traffic lights, some old women coming out of the shops with their packages and moving back into the river of people walking along window-shopping—there wasn't much money for actually buying things. I observed that great heterogeneous mass of people: white people, people not so white, dark people, brown people, and so on and so forth. Montevideo was all this and much more. There were the lame, the well dressed (a few), the ragged (more of these), women with elephantiasis of the legs (I always wondered why there were so many), automobiles, disorder and the hurly burly mess of life.

Miguelito talked a lot. He practically talked my ear off. He spoke about the inevitable dossiers at the bank, about appraisals, about tax shelters, about estimated retirement contributions, about Essar Rays—I didn't understand what kind of rays these could be—which turned out to be S.R.A.'s, that is, Supplemental Retirement Annuities.

Finally I got a word in.

"Tell me, Miguel," I inquired in an off-handed way, "do you happen to know anyone in the Section?"

Miguelito thought for a while, and then, as though he suddenly tuned in to my question, said, "Certainly, I know Gutiérrez. He's been working there for years. I think he's about to retire."

"Would you be able to introduce me to him?"

"Sure thing. What's the matter? Do you have some business to take care of?"

"Well, more or less."

It wasn't easy to get to talk with Gutiérrez. Miguelito, still the same old scatterbrain, forgot to call him or just didn't call him, and besides, he always had an excuse. He had a cold, his wife's mother was sick, Aunt Laura had a broken hip. In other words, that whole series of Uruguayan-style excuses they hand you when friends ask for favors that accrue no benefits to the person who performs the favor, and the request goes in one ear and out the other.

Gutiérrez—Miguelito finally did introduce me to him—was a guy who knew his way around, knew how to deal with all kinds of people, and I could tell right away that he was going to help me and that there would be no problems. He was smoking these little brownish cigarettes, special little Havana cigars, I think they were Moriscos, and was blowing smoke all over the place. Twice he blew smoke practically right in my face, making me cough. His eyes were as shifty as a monkey's, eyes that revealed a certain roguish nature or even something more.

"Miguel Palombo told me that you work with Catalino López," I began.

"I don't know if *work* is the right word, with regard to my activities. Or with regard to our joint activities either. What happens is that we're together and we do something. Catalino is a strange kind of guy. He doesn't like to talk to anybody. Not even to me, and I'm the kind of guy who tries to get people to warm up to me. Once in a while we do exchange a few words, but about something that has to do with the dossiers. When you come right down to it, the dossiers are what hold us all together, whether we belong to the White Party or the Red Party, whether we root for the Peñarol soccer team or the National team."

"Let me tell you what this is all about," I said. "I'd like to get some information about him. We used to be very good friends, but since he got married we don't see each other any more. Could you tell him that I send my regards and ask him to give me a phone call any time at all, that I have something to tell him?"

"Certainly! I'll pass it on tomorrow. And don't worry, I'll have him give you a call."

Gutiérrez made a few more comments on Catalino. He said he thought something was the matter with him. Then he got up, shook my hand and left. I stopped by to see Miguelito for a while. We didn't have anything special to talk about—he was an unimaginative man—just whether they were going to move him out of the filing department, how many goals the National soccer team made—nothing really touched a chord in him. I paid for the coffee, thanked him and left.

At last Catalino called me. It was three o'clock, and the phone in the little vestibule rang. It felt to me as though the vases, the little bottles on shelves from the Gomensoro Pawn Shop, and the statuettes of Italian porcelain all felt the excitement of the moment at hand. I never imagined that Gutiérrez had that much influence. I would certainly have to thank him for the good turn. I'd send him a box of Rhine Gold cookies. For several seconds it was as if I were paralyzed. I couldn't even manage to pick up the receiver even though the phone was ringing as if it were shouting, *Here I am, what do you want?* Finally I picked it up and said *hello*. He said *hello* too. But he was almost unable to speak. You could tell he was greatly troubled and full of anxiety.

"We have got to get together," I said.

"Yes, we have got to get together," he repeated.

"But where?" I asked.

"I... I can't say. I can't think of anything."

"Tell you what. Tomorrow, around five o'clock, you get leave to take a half hour off and we'll meet at a café on Eduardo Acevedo and Uruguay Streets."

"Well... All right," he said, sounding as though he had no alternative.

The café on Eduardo Acevedo and Uruguay is kind of removed from the hubbub of the area the bank is in. Once in a while some old gentleman who needs a shave and is wearing raggedy clothing and has a black hole of a mouth in which you can see only the stumps of some teeth stops by and makes a few comments to someone who might be a niece or a sister or even his wife, in a voice that's loud and uncontrolled because he's hard of hearing. He'll say something unintelligible and poorly articulated which might concern a raffle, or a pressure cooker that's worth a lot of money, or an insurance policy or a purchase on credit, and in the midst of all that incredible verbosity he'll order a capuccino or two which he'll change to three and then change back to two and then he'll slurp and slurp and loudly swish it through his toothless mouth. He is like a bit of cosmic dust, without a fixed path in outer space, fled from that collision zone which is the esplanade of the bank, where hundreds of elderly people in every physical and spiritual state collide like molecules of gas while trying to collect their retirement funds.

The district in which the bank is located is unique, and with its diversity of pawnshops, of shops that sell candy, washing machines, sneakers and foodstuffs with ineffable aromas that emanate from their dark depths, brings to mind the spasmodic disorder of life in the Orient.

He showed up at five o'clock, looking like a wet chicken emerging from that world of effervescent human activity. There was nothing left of the boy who used to come to the café on Sierra Street. He looked at me and could barely manage a smile. His hair had turned white, and he even seemed to tremble somewhat. Two years had changed him completely.

I sat down and so did he. I ordered two coffees while the ragged, toothless old man slurped his tall capuccino as loudly as some kind of savage. We didn't have time to drink our coffee. Suddenly, with all the violence of a tornado, Fatty flew in through the side door, made a beeline for our table, stared a hole through Catalino and made him sit through an entire harangue:

"So you're playing dirty pool with me, are you? What are you doing now? Playing around with your old cronies again, eh? You still think the atmosphere of a saloon in constructive and that life is nothing but wine, women and song? Or playing kissy-face with your bimbos? All right now... You just get up this very instant and come with me right now," she said in a voice of thunder. "And you, pardon us," she added, but in a tone of voice that was entirely devoid of courtesy.

Catalino stood up without opening his mouth—like a meek little lamb—, automatically offered his arm to Fatty and went out with her through the back door. He didn't say one word to me. I was left there meditating about who knows what, and couldn't come up with any ideas.

Still and all, I didn't give up after that incident. I still kept them under surveillance. When you get right down to it, I don't know what was biting me, what kept pushing me to stand up for him. Catalino had always been a good guy, always willing to do a favor for someone, and he was a real friend to his friends, so I just couldn't allow this to happen to him.

When Gutiérrez called me and told me that Catalino was ill and that he hadn't been coming to the bank, I swung into action again. I called him up but, as usual, the phone was answered by Fatty.

"What do you want?" she asked me gruffly.

"To see how Catalino's doing, ma'am," I said fearlessly.

"He's sick." She said this as though she were pleased.

"Well, give him regards from his pal Juancho and tell him that I'd like to come over and see him."

"That won't be possible at this time. Some other time, maybe," she muttered and hung up.

The next day I got this great idea. You can see I was always thinking. I stood at the corner of Benito Blanco and Pereira, and I saw Fatty leave. She got into her car, started the engine and away she went. I took advantage of the situation and slipped into the Costa Azul Building like a ghost. I had been waiting on that corner for more than an hour.

I got into the elevator and pressed the button. The ride to the ninth floor seemed to take an eternity; I could feel Fatty's hot breath on my neck, but I made myself calm down. After all, I had seen her leave, so there was nothing to fear. At last I got to the ninth floor and stepped into the hallway. It was completely dark there, and I couldn't find the light switch. Finally I saw it and was able to read the name on the door. It was apartment 901 and the name was *Pintos-López Family*. Contrary to custom, her surname came before his. I rang the doorbell and waited. Then I heard a voice.

"Who is it?" the voice said with evident sorrow and fear.

"It's me, Juancho."

"Who?"

"Juancho."

"Oh! It's you," he mumbled. "Just a minute."

Catalino came up to his side of the door and began to talk without opening the door.

"Look, Juancho, I can't open the door because Mar¢ia Teresa keeps it locked and takes the key with her. She doesn't want me to open the door for any one because there are all kinds of nasty people around."

"How are you feeling?" I inquired.

"Not too well. I don't feel well at all. I still think about the old gang at the café."

"Then why don't you stop in?"

"What can I tell you...? I can't."

"Can't you do anything?"

"No, I can't. I'm not allowed."

I was absorbed in this conversation and didn't notice that the elevator had started up again, that it had now stopped, and that the door was opening and Fatty was getting out.

"Wasn't I just saying that this Catalino is going to give me a heart attack with his old cronies and his impudence?" Then she furiously inquired of me, "What are you doing here?"

"I was talking with Catalino through the door."

"Don't you know he's sick and that I've forbidden him to speak? Friends... You're just like dogs; you recognize each other and track one another down with your noses. Thank heavens at least something told me to check up on him. I had a feeling someone was hanging around the neighborhood."

"Look, I can understand your apprehension, but as an old friend I have a right to find out how he's doing."

"If you're such a good friend you'll wait for him to get better and, since you insist so much, we'll invite you over and you'll be able to come here for an evening. But for now, goodbye and do not disturb Catalino any more without permission."

Then she opened the door, walked inside, and slammed the door. I could hear her say, "You're a naughty boy. Talking through the door like that when I've told you not to answer the door for anyone. Get to bed now, and be quick about it," she shouted in a voice that now sounded to me more like that of a husky he-man than that of a woman.

* * *

When Fatty actually called, I couldn't believe my ears. I never imagined she would call me. She even sounded polite, or at least she had that minimal courtesy that a masculine woman can sometimes have. She was inviting Gabriel and me to have coffee at their apartment. I didn't know what to say. She said we could come over on Saturday at about eight o'clock.

On Saturday the eighteenth Gabriel stopped by to pick me up, and we headed out to Catalino's place. The weather was nippy, with the chill of the first days of May in the Southern Hemisphere, and we arrived at Benito Blanco Street anxious to warm ourselves at a nice oven or room heater. We went up to the ninth floor. Having been there already, I had no trouble finding the door of apartment 901, and I rang the bell. About a minute went by and there were no signs of life in the apartment. It looked as though no one were home. I rang once more and the door opened in a way that seemed automatic. Framed in the doorway by a violet light from within the apartment, Fatty's form stood out in all its immensity.

This time, more than ever before, she produced an impression of tremendous masculinity, of a masculinity that might be called arrogant and even crude. There was something about her that brought to mind a heavyweight boxer. An imposing jaw and a nose that was flattened out over a mouth with fleshy, lustful lips. She was wearing jeans and a shirt with large red checks.

"Come in," she said. "Here's your friend," she added, pointing to him seated at the table.

"We wanted to have this little get-together to show you we have nothing against his friends." She made this announcement in a tone of voice that was gruff but was attempting to convey a trace of amiability.

The apartment was furnished in an indescribable manner. Catalino's chair was small and low, and you could only see his head and a few centimeters of torso emerging above the level of the table. Hers was high and massive and allowed her to look down on everyone else. Gabriel's and mine, as well as one extra chair, were of normal size.

"Be seated," she said, and Catalino nodded in assent.

On the walls, which were painted an intense blue-violet, instead of paintings there were a few photographs of heavily-muscled men looking like Arnold Schwartzenegger, a Tarzan of the Apes in glorious full color, and some hairy gorillas and orangutans with menacingly furious eyes. And on one very low, very small table, there was a sculpture of a wrestler trying to pin an exceedingly ugly simian. At one end of the living room was a sofa-bed and a sort of large wooden case which could not be clearly identified, perhaps a piece of furniture, a coffin or a record player.

"I suppose you'll accept a cup of coffee," she said in a tone of voice that was intended to be cordial.

"Yes, ma'am," I said.

"Don't call me *ma'am*. Call me Orion. That business of giving people titles annoys me," she explained.

We looked at one another and said nothing. Catalino, down there in his little chair, didn't dare to intervene.

"I'm going to go and make the coffee," she said. Then, looking at our friend, added, "See that you don't throw caution to the winds and run off at the mouth."

In the brief time in which she was out of the room, Catalino made a pathetic attempt at a look of friendship that perhaps was intended to tell us something like, "Well, boys, that's the way things are. It can't be helped."

Almost immediately Fatty returned with four demitasse cups. It was obvious that everything had been prepared in advance. She didn't want to waste a single second.

"Here you are: a good mocha blended with Colombian, the way we like it."

There was a dead silence. I absently ran my eyes once more over the apes on the walls, and no one said a word.

"As you can see, we live very well," she commented, finally breaking the silence.

"So it seems," my friend said.

"And what about you? How are you doing?" I inquired, looking at Catalino. "How are things with you?"

"With me...?"

"Just a moment," Fatty Orion interrupted. "You just let me explain everything to them."

"I just wanted to say..." Catalino mumbled again.

"You didn't want to say anything. I know what your friends should be told," Orion commanded.

Catalino lowered his eyes and said nothing.

"This gentleman, if that is the correct term, is a very rebellious person and pays no attention to anything. Imagine! From the time we contracted matrimony I haven't been able to get him to stop listening to the soccer matches, the games played by that damned Peñarol team," she said in a tone that strained to be correct, but in the end had taken on a certain edge of violence.

From the coffee table in the living room I was able to see through the partially opened door into the bedroom. The bed—that ancient setting for making love in a hundred different ways and in which one then snored peacefully—was unmade, and the sheets were visible, sheets that looked pink, that transported one to the realms of fantasy, of tenderness and caresses.

"He's always wasting so much time on soccer. Broadcasts from the stadium, broadcasts on radio and on television, the players this, that and the other, Semino this, Miraglia that, and on and on and on. And that's without even mentioning his precious tango recordings, because I've put an end to that nonsense. He was driving me up the wall with those composers like Canaro, D'Agostino and who knows how many more. Now he can listen only to Beethoven, Bach or Brahms in this house, and nothing else. He says they bore him. Well, fine, he doesn't have to listen to anything then. I'm too kind to him by not forcing him to listen to my favorite composers because, as far as I'm concerned, the three great B's of Germany make me sigh, transport me to heaven, make me lose my reason. But you know what Catalino is, what your fine friend is: a loser. You hear me: a real loser. And it's all his mother's fault because when she was alive she didn't know how to bring him up properly. That's why I have to take him in hand. I have to guide him in everything. And I don't know how long it's going to take me," Fatty concluded with satisfaction.

Catalino looked straight ahead without attempting the least defense.

The conversation continued in this way, with harsh, exceedingly harsh, criticism of Catalino and his lack of responsibility as a member of the family. All this time he kept quiet, sitting in his little chair and staring at the floor, looking as though he were imploring someone to do something, but what that something was, we couldn't decipher.

The apes in the photographs stared at us with fire in their eyes and gave the impression that they were trying to break free from the pictures on the wall and attack us.

Fatty Orion finally turned red in the face and was having difficulty breathing, so prolonged was her diatribe against poor Catalino. From time to time she had been practically shouting.

"You are a loser. You don't know how to behave, and I'm going to have to tighten the screws more, you shameless wretch. You're getting off easy now because your friends are here," she said, and then added in the worst tone possible, "you driveling simpleton, you're no good to me for anything anymore."

The conversation was bogging down. Orion was on the verge of hysteria. The apes and the body builders appeared to be in a frenzy, and I believe that Gabriel and I stood up at precisely the same instant. We said we had to go, we shook hands, and left. Catalino's hand was trembling. Fatty Orion's hand felt like the hand of a truck driver, it was so big and its grip so firm. We opened the door to the hallway. The woman was a little calmer, but she still appeared to be irritated.

Once out in the hallway, we experienced a sense of freedom and could breathe more easily. We immediately began to walk down the stairs; we couldn't even stand the idea of waiting for the elevator. We needed to get away from that oppressive atmosphere as soon as possible. As we descended, we heard a sort of howl coming from the apartment.

* * *

A month later, Catalino sent us a letter from prison. He asked us to visit him there. He said there were a lot of things he wanted to explain. We never got up the courage to go.

OLD FRIENDS

I don't know why, but just before my seventieth birthday I began to think about—no, it was more than that—to burrow feverishly into my childhood and early adolescence. It was summertime, and I'd sit in back of the house those mornings, sipping *maté* in peace and quiet, without a care in the world. Gazing at the malvón bushes I had planted two years earlier, gradually, irresistibly, my thoughts returned to the past. I was going through a period of nostalgia. "Is this what growing old is all about," I wondered. "Just yearning for the past, reliving old times?" Still and all, now that I think of it, this was really nothing new. I'd been doing that for years: sitting down and thinking of the old days, wanting to reconstruct the past, searching for something in that past that I couldn't find in the present, and that I surely was not going to find in the future.

Lately there had been one memory in particular that continually preyed on my mind. It brought me back to my childhood, and the image of Lázaro, Lázaro Dorón, once again took shape in my mind's eye. I would spend hours with him when I was a child. We played statues, marbles and paddle ball. We had fights, sure, and we yelled at each other, but we were always friends, great friends.

It wasn't only his character and his intelligence that I admired but his background too. Lázaro wasn't like the rest of the kids. He came from Europe, Russia, to be exact. From some village in Russia where it was cold and snow-covered practically all year long. A place like that stirred my youthful imagination. He seemed different from all my other friends. He wasn't like Juan, or Alvaro, or Gastoncito, the other kids in the neighborhood. That's the reason—the air of mystery that he radiated—that I always felt more like talking to him, playing with him, than with the others. My childish mind still seethed with curiousity. I wanted to unravel the secrets of the European world that hid behind every one of his gestures, the way he looked at you, even the way he smiled. I found all this mysterious and at times unfathomable.

One day—I don't know why—it occurred to me to ask him what language he used when he spoke with his parents. It was very clear: he told me he spoke Yiddish with them. Right then and there I wanted to learn some Yiddish, but he stopped me in my tracks and said, "If you want to learn an important language, choose Hebrew. I know a little, because I'm studying it at the Hebrew Day School, and I'll be able to teach you some too." I'll still remember the first letters—*aleph, beth, gimmel*—and the first phrases: *Hiney ha-shikun she-lanu. Dinah ovedet ba-ginah...*

We used to spend winter afternoons—those rainy, grey afternoons of the Montevideo winter—in my living room. He'd bring his little Hebrew textbook and would be pleased as Punch to teach me. We took a break from studying every once in a while and played a game. Once, I don't remember how it happened, a little movie projector fell into our hands. It was the most primitive machine you could imagine. It was hand operated, and the light came from a tiny kerosene lamp. I remember that we turned off the lights in the room and then deliriously tried to project the images of a Charlie Chaplin film that we got through a friend. We would spend hours on end attempting it, but succeeded only in seeing some motionless image, some still picture of Charlie. Still and all, although you may find it hard to believe, it was a triumph. In the midst of the strong smell of

62

kerosene, we were entranced watching the motionless picture of Chaplin against the wall. To this day I am haunted by that kerosene. Whenever I detect the odor of kerosene, at home or anywhere else, I unavoidably return to the days of my childhood and Lázaro.

After a few months I got to know quite a few phrases in Hebrew. I felt as though I were walking on air when I used these phrases to converse a little with Lázaro. It gave me the feeling that I had stolen something important out of that world of strange ideas and values that he represented. His mother was a very nice woman and gave me little cookies she said were typical of her country or a piece of cake filled with delicious creams and chocolates. His father was kind of gruff and rarely spoke. I got the impression that he didn't think it was such a great idea for his son to be friends with a *goy*, as I later learned they called us Christians.

One day I met an elderly gentleman who came to Lázaro's house on Monday's. He was a very unusual person. He dressed all in black, wore a circular, very wide-brimmed hat and had a full beard. It was a long, pointed beard that made him look like a medieval knight. If someone had asked me for my impression at that time, I'd have said the old gentleman was coming from some kind of temple or some holy place where serenity, respect and austerity reigned; from a world in which greatness of spirit and a love for all that is unknown rules supreme. What's more, I'd have said that he was a man who had just arrived from the regions of mystery, from the beyond, to spend a few hours —perhaps distressing hours—with men of flesh and blood, with those men who never agreed on anything. Well, I wasn't long in learning who this good man was and what he did. He was Lázaro's grandfather and was the rabbi of part of the Ashkenazic community of the city. This accounted for his serious mien, his grave circumspection. Lázaro explained to me that he wore the garb of the Mizrachi sect and that he was a very serious-minded man.

One morning that I can hardly remember, the Doróns moved out of the neighborhood. They moved away, and there is still a void in my memory that I have not succeeded in filling. What I do remember is that a few days before moving, Lázaro's parents had this grand celebration for him. It was a family affair, a party that to me seemed secret and mysterious, and that even had a special name, a name that sounded magical to me: *Bar Mitzvah*. He explained a little about it to me. He told me that from that day on his parents considered him a full-fledged man, and he said he was sorry he hadn't invited me.

After that, life began to pass by very rapidly, this life that leads us all along such different paths and moves at a bewildering speed, turning young men into adults and adults into old men and who knows what else.

A year ago, when I made up my mind to seek Lázaro out, at first I wondered if I might not be suffering from some malady. What purpose could I have in wanting to find him? The past was the past, and I couldn't comprehend how that unhealthy obsession to reconstruct it originated in me, particularly in the person of Lázaro Dorón, whose image had remained for so many long years in my memory even though he himself no longer existed in my real life. Why was he so important to my past? It's true that we were great friends as children, yes. And it's true that there was something mysterious, unfathomable, about him and his family. But why now, almost sixty years later, was I torturing myself with the idea—with the need—of finding him?

Be that as it were, I couldn't fight it: that compulsion to see Dorón once more, to speak with him, to reminisce about the past. So I rolled up my sleeves and set to work. The first thing I did, that very day on which I made up my mind, was to check for his name or that of any other Dorón in the telephone book. What a disappointment! Not a single Dorón was listed. Later I looked through an old Century Directory, the last one that had come out, but to no avail. There were no Doróns. Being a man of willpower, as well a methodical planner, I drew up a plan of action. I would have to talk to every rabbi in the city and find out if they had him on their membership lists. Then, if this failed, I would initiate a search in greater depth. I would visit the most aged Jews of the community—in the Old City of Montevideo and in Villa Muñoz, two areas of substantial Jewish population—and make some inquiries. I had no doubt that one of them would have known the elder Dorón, the old rabbi of the Mizrachi sect, and would be able to provide me with some information on the whereabouts of the family and, ultimately, of Lázaro.

I did a great deal of walking. I visited each and every synagogue. While waiting to speak to the rabbi, I would become ecstatic as I gazed at the interior of the temples. They were different from Catholic churches. There was a feeling of greater seriousness in them. I was deeply impressed by a kind of austerity which reigned over all. Up in front, the simple nobility of the ark which contained the Torah—the scrolls of sacred writ, the Five Books of Moses—completely dominated the uncluttered surroundings, lending a note of ineffable grandeur. Facing the ark, the silent purity of the *bimah* reflected the mystery of religious meditation. On the walls, here and there, the pure whiteness of the tiny lights traced the stylized outlines of the *menorah*, recalling the deeds of the Maccabees. Each time, I waited for a while and then the rabbi came to meet me. The answer to my question was always the same: Dorón was unknown. There was a point at which I even began to suspect that Lázaro wasn't Jewish after all, that my mind was going. In spite of my failure up to that point, I pressed on with my search. I didn't know exactly what to do during the first days. I visited as many Jewish shops as I could locate and spoke with the owners, always asking the same question: had they ever heard of Dorón. The answer was always the same. No one had ever heard of Dorón, the Mizrachi rabbi, and certainly not of his grandson, my old friend.

One day I had a brilliant idea. It occurred to me that Lázaro and his family might have moved across the River Plate to Buenos Aires. One autumn afternoon I took the brief flight from Montevideo to the Argentine capital. I checked into what might prove to be the nerve center, the solution to my problem: I rented a room at the Wertheim, a Jewish hotel on Tucumán Street. You can't imagine how comfortable I felt there. People were speaking Yiddish everywhere, or, if not Yiddish, it would be Spanish with a Yiddish accent. I was enthralled to hear all those elderly Jews speaking about their pasts in Europe and about their initial ups and downs in Argentina.

Almost all were elderly Jewish men who, each afternoon

toward evening, pushed the armchairs in the hotel lobby around to form a sort of ring. They constituted a warm circle of friends in the mood for a couple of hours of *shmoozing*, as they called it, of chewing the fat. One of them was very old, maybe almost ninety years old, and his voice, because it was cracked and weak, didn't allow me to understand anything, especially if he was speaking Yiddish, of course. I had better luck understanding the others, since they spoke with clearer voices and often inserted entire phrases or sentences in Spanish. There was one Sephardic Jew in the group—he was originally from Turkey—who got together with his coreligionists once in a while. Then they all spoke in Spanish, for his benefit, and my ears pricked up and I really enjoyed listening to the tales these men told. One spoke of his childhood in Poland, another of his youth in Russia, another of his grandparents in Lithuania. I spent hours, in my chair, not too far removed from the group, playing dumb and listening to them. It was like being present at a performance in which the mysteries of man and of all creation were revealed, because, as far as I was concerned, these men were exotic beings who came from mysterious realms.

A time came in which I had almost forgotten about Lázaro, about my mission to Buenos Aires. All day I looked forward to the evening and going down to the lobby to make myself comfortable in my armchair and await the never-failing conversations. The autumnal atmosphere lent the perfect note. Outside, the grey chill of fall, people going and coming along Tucumán Street; inside, the cozy warmth of the hotel and the elderly Jews gradually joining the little group. But one afternoon, as though I were awakening from a dream, I finally said to myself: "You're out of your mind, Pedro. You came here to search for Lázaro, didn't you?"

I didn't have the heart to ask any questions of those good men. Instead, I decided to start strolling around the neighborhood to stop in at the shops along Tucumán as well as the side streets—Junín, Paso, Larrea, etc.—in other words, the streets of the "ghetto," as people in Buenos Aires called the district. The names alone of the stores brought reminiscences of strange things, of cities dreamed of in my imagination, of enchanted lands: Koldonski Notions, Malamud Clothiers, Goldberg

Bazaar, Chicurel Tailors... At first I was too timid to do anything more than look at the store windows as though I were merely killing time. Later, more confident, more at home in the district, I took to standing still for a while and looked toward the inside of the store. In every store there were great piles of merchandise, and there were people moving packages or boxes from one place to another. Each store swarmed with activity and was filled with objects. My eyes were drawn toward the back of the store, to a pile of multicolored towels or of bright fabrics, and I wanted to imagine that behind all that sat some venerable Hebrew sage counting coins or lost in mysterious meditations, in those meditations I was then trying to comprehend but which kept evading me. How happy and secure was that life among packages and colors and perfumes and merchandise! My entire soul became intoxicated at all that. I imagined I was traveling through time, going back to Antiquity, to Asiatic bazaars filled with infinite marvels and mysteries. What a contrast all this was to the rude life of the Spanish immigrants who always did business in dirty little stores filled with foodstuffs, with redolent codfish, salamis gone sour or rancid cheeses!

The Jews were finer, more polished, but also more mysterious people. They knew how to live like gentlemen among luxuries. This is because they came from the East. They were men straight out of *The Thousand and One Nights*, and they were privy to and masters of the great secrets of existence. How I envied them!

One day I actually got up the courage to enter a notions store. I don't know how or why. I bought a spool of twine, and used the opportunity to ask a question in an off-handed manner.

"You wouldn't happen to know of a furniture dealer by the name of Dorón living in the neighborhood, would you?"

That business about a furniture dealer came to me out of the blue. Who knows how it happened. It was a way of shifting the conversation in a natural way toward business, something that made my question sound normal. The answer was negative. There was no Dorón on that block.

The following day I went into other places of business, and later I became accustomed to doing this and went into others and still others and finally it was easy. People say that doing something often builds confidence; it's the truth, let me tell you. I covered the entire ghetto. I even went into a deli that emitted a wonderful aroma, and ordered a bagel and lox. But I didn't find any Doróns.

Traveling home on Argentine Airlines, I was depressed. The possibility of locating Lázaro and reliving the past with him was dissolving, slipping through my fingers. Then the worst thought occurred to me: my old friend might possibly be in New York or in Los Angeles or in any one of those great cities of the United States which lure men of enterprise. Or, what would be even more serious, he might have gone to live in Israel.

* * *

When I moved into my new apartment on Brazil Avenue and Chucarro Street, I was struck by my neighbors' names. Almost all of them had foreign names. I checked, just in case, but there was no Dorón. The tenants on my floor were very pleasant, but only said hello to me and then went on their way. I figured they were Jewish by their name, Levinski, and this made me feel great. I couldn't help associating what was Jewish with my memories of Lázaro; that's why I was so elated.

From all appearances, the only people who lived in the apartment were the Levinski couple and the maid, a girl with Indian features who went out every morning to get the milk. So I was perplexed one day in the fall when I saw, from behind, an old man who had come out of the Levinski apartment and was taking the elevator. I don't know why, but the presence of the old gentleman getting into the elevator really caught my attention and plunged me into thought. How was it that I had not seen this man before? He was presumably a tenant himself of the next-door apartment and maybe—or rather, without a doubt—was the father of one of the Levinskis. Through the large window that faced the avenue, I looked at, but did not really see, the fallen leaves of autumn accumulating on the the the sidewalks. Meanwhile, my imagination soared. At last I made up my mind to keep an eye on the old fellow to see what he was like and who he was.

Several days later, at the same time, noon, I took up my position on the landing and waited for what seemed an eternity for the man to come out of the apartment. Finally the door of the Levinski apartment opened, and a slow-moving, dark figure emerged. He was a man of my own age but in worse physical condition. It was obvious that he was in poor health. He was bald and had large protruding ears like Lázaro's. He went downstairs, and I stood there turning the matter over in my mind. Couldn't he be Lázaro? The human physiognomy changes a great deal in fifty or sixty years. Time can convert a bright, fresh face into an unrecognizable mass of wrinkles. This could have happened to my good friend Lázaro.

While I was trying to figure out a stratagem for finding out who the elderly man was, something unforeseeable happened. Mrs. Levinski came to my door one afternoon to discuss a problem involving the apartment house roof. She was very congenial and exhibited that vivacity and charm that refined Jewish women have. As she left, she explained that the old fellow, who had worked very hard in his lifetime, was not in the best of health. As a token of friendship, she left her calling card with me and told me to call her if I needed anything. Our relationship as neighbors, then, began on a wonderful note. The calling card read:

Salomon Levinski
Rose D. Levinski

The letter D in her name sent a chill along my spine. I imagined that it concealed the surname Dorón and with it the entire past that I was fervently seeking to relive. To think that I had covered so much territory trying to find Dorón without the least success, and now the Lord seemed to be presenting him to me on a silver platter...Because I now took for granted that the good man was Lázaro Dorón.

For days on end I wracked my brain trying to find a way of learning what my neighbor's maiden name might be. Unfortunately, I didn't come up with a thing. I couldn't find the way to solve the problem. Fortunately, just when I frantically began to lose all hope of acquiring the information, a miracle occurred. Mrs. Levinski came to my apartment again to talk about the matter of the dampness on the ceiling, and—talking about this, that and the other thing—I came up with a way of asking the question.

"You wouldn't be one of the Dubinski family, by any chance, would you? I'm asking because I saw that your maiden name starts with a D, and I once knew a boy named Dubinski when I was a student."

I realized all at once that this was the most elegant way to broach the matter, and I was satisfied. It would have been indiscreet to have asked about her last name directly. The results bore me out. Mrs. D. Levinski looked at me with the satisfaction that comes from knowing that the person you're speaking with cares enough to want to know little details about your life. So, in spite of that sixth sense the Jewish people have, she fell into the trap. Vanity got the better of her.

"No, I'm a Dorón," she said with vehemence and pride.

I felt as though my head were spinning and couldn't think of a thing to say.

"Are you feeling tired?" the good woman asked me. She must have noticed something peculiar in my appearance.

"No," I managed to respond, trying to recover from the tremendous shock. "It's just a passing indisposition. If you don't mind, we can get back to the matter of the ceiling tomorrow. All right?"

As soon as Mrs. Dorón left, I fell heavily into the old, dark green velvet easy chair that had been in my parents' home and which I still held on to. I began to think. My mind began to race at an incredible speed. Without intending to, I returned to my childhood and to the days spent with Lázaro. Fate was now offering me the opportunity I had been desperately seeking. My friend Lázaro—the good man could be no one else—was now within my reach. I would soon be able to speak with him face to face.

I had recovered from the happy shock by the next day. When Mrs. Levinski finished talking about the dampness coming from the roof and was rising to leave, I gave the appearance of clearing my throat, mumbled something inconsequential, and returned to the fray.

"Excuse me... The white-haired gentleman who goes out at noon... Is he your father?" I asked.

"Why, yes. He is. He's aged a great deal lately, gotten old

70

before his time. His memory is almost completely gone," she explained.

During the night I laid my plans for approaching Lázaro, because there was no longer the shadow of a doubt that this was Lázaro. The following afternoon, in accordance with the plan I had devised, I rang the Doróns' doorbell. Mrs. Levinski opened the door for me in person and immediately, in the most cordial manner, asked me to step inside.

"Now I'm the one who has to speak with you," I said.

"Go on, please," she said.

"I've been thinking… There's this really good company that could repair the roof at a pretty good price," I explained.

The pretext worked very well. We continued talking for several minutes and shared our ideas on the dampness problem. During the conversation, the elderly gentleman came into the living room. I looked at him very carefully and was able to confirm almost to my complete satisfaction that this was indeed Lázaro. Time had left its inevitable traces on that face and especially on that mind. It was obvious that he didn't recognize people very well. He greeted me amiably and took a seat in a fine, dark leather arm chair.

"He's completely exhausted," his daughter whispered. "But he loves to meet new people. It wouldn't bother you if he stays here with us, would it?"

"No, not at all," I affirmed with the greatest emphasis.

"Daddy, this is our next-door neighbor, Mr. López." She said this loudly so that the good man could hear her. Then she immediately turned to me and said, "Mr. López, this is my father, Lázaro Dorón."

The conversation about the dampness came to an end, and then we began to make small talk, the small talk that people always resort to when we don't want to or are unable to become involved in serious matters. Things like, "the cost of living is high," "the weather is bad," "the summer will be rainy," and so on. At one point I attempted to exchange a couple of words with Lázaro, after she had stepped out of the room for a few moments. (She had asked if I would like a brandy, and I had most gladly agreed to let her go and bring it.) I stared at Lázaro once more, and I think I uttered some words or another of no importance. I didn't have the courage to get down to cases. I was trembling as a boy does in the presence of his first love.

"Have you folks been living here long?" I managed to say to break the silence.

The good man didn't hear me very well and responded that the winter was bad for him. Deep within me I was quivering with emotion. Here was Lázaro right in front of my nose, and I found myself unable to say a word. I couldn't get myself to speak of the past with him, that past we had shared like brothers when we were children. Scenes of the happiest moments of my life flashed across my mind. I saw myself with the little kerosene movie projector, with the homemade ball, sitting at the table in Lázaro's house, in front of a lamp, studying Hebrew...So many other things.

His daughter was taking long with the drinks. The minute hand on the clock kept moving, but I was unable to take advantage of the opportunity that had fallen into my lap like pennies from heaven; I didn't identify myself. The man looked at me and repeated, "The winter is bad for me."

Finally, the daughter arrived with a little tray holding two glasses of cognac. Now, I hardly ever used to touch cognac, and even less so at that age, but the anxiety and dejection I was feeling were so strong that I eagerly accepted the cognac and drained the glass in one gulp.

I stayed a little while longer. Then I stood up, shook hands with her and then with Lázaro. My friend's hand was cold and clammy. I looked into his eyes once more, said goodbye and left.

That same night I heard a great deal of activity going on in the Levinski apartment. At twelve-thirty, Mr. Levinski himself came and asked if he could use the phone. He said he was sorry to bother me, but their phone was out of order, and they needed one urgently. The old fellow had suffered a stroke and was unable to move.

Some weeks went by. The good man had been saved from death but was very ill. At night the poor fellow moaned like an animal in pain. Since we all knew each other pretty well by now—we were no longer strangers—I arranged to go and see him as soon as he got a little better. Now I was feeling confident that I would be able to really speak with him and reminisce about the past.

One day—it was almost summertime—they let me go in and see him. I just sat there watching him for a long time. The poor fellow stammered terribly, but he managed to communicate. Then there was a moment in which he looked at me and said:

"You know, you look very familiar."

This moved me so deeply that I was unable to say anything. I felt something like a knot tightening around my throat. I wanted to tell him who I was and start talking about the past with him, but I just couldn't do it. A moment passed, and I finally managed to speak.

"Could be," was all I managed to say, and then I was silent again.

He died within a few days. I went to the funeral parlor. There weren't many people there. The casket rested on a pair of low supports. The atmosphere was subdued. In the back of the room were two simple candelabra and the Star of David. A ribbon draped over the coffin bore the name Lázaro Dorón.

I had indeed found Lázaro. But it was too late. I was left alone with the memories of our past.

In one corner of the room a middle-aged man was grieving over my friend's death. He suddenly looked up at me and said:

"He wasn't just the *shoyhet*, the man who kosher-killed our chickens. He was a dear friend. And now he's gone."

All I could think of saying was, "Yes, he's gone."

THE TABLE

Mr. Valbuena briefly explained what his duties in the firm would be, showed him to the little work table he had been assigned—there was nothing better at the time, and the boy had to take what they offered—and handed him his first invoice pad.

Johnny, who was rather shy, lowered his head and, following the man's instructions, filled out his first invoice. The woman who occupied the desk on his left—he thought she looked Brazilian—glanced at him several times and finally decided to speak to him.

"Is this your first job?" She asked this with a certain air of superiority born of experience with the firm.

"Yes," was all Johnny could answer, his voice cracking.

A first job is like one's first woman. Johnny didn't know how he would fit in. He anxiously waited for twelve noon to roll around so he could go home to be with his mother.

"How did it go, Johnny?" Mrs. Hernández demanded as soon as the boy returned from work.

"Not bad, Mom," he answered tremulously. "What I don't like, though, is the desk they gave me. It's not actually a desk;

it's just a little table made of wood from a kerosene crate. They told me it'd be only for a little while. I always dreamed of having a nice desk when I began to work, but no such luck."

"Don't you worry, Johnny. They'll give you something; you'll see. You're barely sixteen. You're young. For now, working on invoices at a little table made from a kerosene crate isn't such a terrible thing. Besides, fourteen pesos a month isn't a bad salary. If only your father were alive... He'd be so proud of you!"

The first year went by and he had no complaints. Mercanti, Inc. did well that year and gave him a few pesos as a bonus as well as a raise of one peso. The only thing that annoyed him was their not trading in the little table for a real desk. He began his second year right there in the invoicing corner, facing the wall, beside the Brazilian woman.

Then came 1930 with its global Depression which threatened incipient industry and small business. Mercanti, Inc. laid off several employees, but Johnny remained. With the threat of being fired hanging over his head during the bleak period of the crisis, he made do with the little pine table for several years. At home that table and his need for a desk were taboo as subjects of conversation.

Only the senior clerk from Brazil and a sporty gentleman named Gorostizaga were left in the Invoice Department. Gorostizaga seemed to have no interest other than soccer and the Peñarol team. One day in 1938, Johnny, who finally lost some of his timidity, had a long conversation with Gorostizaga, who was hard of hearing, and attempted to bring up the subject of the little table and ascertain whether it would be exchanged for a desk. The man had difficulty understanding him and continued speaking about soccer. He felt the Peñarol team was a shoo-in for the championship.

Some months later, right before the beginning of World War II, Johnny screwed up the courage to say a few words to the senior clerk from Brazil and asked her if by some chance she thought they would get rid of the table. The brunette brazenly looked him up and down and said, "Look, kid, what you need is a woman, not a desk." Then she lit a cigarette and continued working.

When the Second World War broke out in 1939, the Brazilian

woman was fired for reasons that were never disclosed, and shortly after this Gorostizaga died. The company took this opportunity to remove the two desks and put in their place some filing cabinets filled with correspondence that had been in the basement. Since there was little activity, they did not hire additional help; Johnny, no longer a little boy, was stuck with all the invoicing work.

Those were years of monotony, almost of desolation. Life was an eternal routine that the poor fellow bore without realizing it and without rebelling. For him, Sundays in the spring and summer meant nothing more than a stroll along the lake in Rodó Park from which he would return home early. Sundays in fall and winter represented only the soccer game and reading the paper. And in between were the weekdays, the inevitable week with its invoices and more invoices, the inescapable rising at seven, the habitual washing of face, teeth, feet or whatever, the indispensable breakfast. And always, day after day, the same trip by trolley car and the identical topography: Rivera Street, Colonia Street, the squalidly narrow confines of the office, the hermetically grey walls, Colonia Street, Rivera Street, home once more, night and sleep.

Under the glass top of his desk, Gorostizaga had left a photograph of the victorious Peñarol team of '38 and one of the legendary tango singer, good old Carlos Gardel, wearing his grey slouch hat. Just before the desk was removed, Johnny had been bold enough to remove the pictures, and later hung them on the wall in his corner. Whenever he was depressed, thinking about being stuck with the little table, he would lift his eyes to gaze with undeclining fervor at the colors of his soccer club, since he too was a fan of the gold-and-blacks.

It was 1940; Johnny was now in the full bloom of his manhood. He was thirty years old and was acutely aware of the emptiness of his life, an emptiness which was the product of the isolation in which he lived. There was a blonde young woman he admired from afar. She used to get off the trolley number 31 at his stop, but he never found the courage to speak to her. "Why take a chance on being rejected," he would tell himself in his interior monologues.

Valbuena would often come to the office because of some invoicing problem, and Johnny would tell him from time to time that he felt a bit cramped in that corner or that his surroundings were far from attractive. Valbuena, his mind always on business, paid him no heed. On one occasion he seemed inclined to converse with John, but it lasted only a few seconds and the conversation dealt with the illness of his mother, who had a stone in her left kidney, more than with anything else. It was all over without Johnny's being able to mount a frontal attack.

The War came to a close, and John had been with Mercanti, Inc. for seventeen years. The initial postwar years were trying and left no place for even thinking about desks or new equipment. The firm, which had converted much of its capital into liquid assets and had just suffered heavy financial losses, found it necessary to face a new era, new competitors, new marketing methods, and there was Johnny ready to lend a helping hand to his superiors. He was no longer the young lad he had been in the 1930s, but he still lived like an adolescent. He still loved and respected his mother just as much as when he was fifteen.

In 1949 they took on a new invoice clerk, a man of some forty years of age, who had a great deal of experience from previous work with other firms in the city. They set him up in Johnny's office and brought him the desk that had belonged to Gorostizaga. This wounded John deeply. He, who for so many years had looked forward to a decent desk, found himself stepped on by Valbuena and the sons of Mercanti, who now ran all aspects of the firm. But he held his tongue. He kept his mouth shut, stifling his emotions, and continued to work, even outdoing himself to demonstrate his love for the company.

With the increase in business that came with the following year, the Mercantis decided to do some renovating. They gave the walls a fresh coat of paint, purchased new desks for several different clerks and even installed the latest Marelli electric fans in some of the offices. Billy Mercanti, the youngest of Don Vicente's sons, took on a Paraguayan friend he used to hang around with on the streets, and put him to work in invoicing right next to John. He took the opportunity to reinstall the Brazilian woman's desk, which, even though it was nothing to write home about, was much better than the humble little pine table that Johnny still used. The next few weeks were bitter for him. His mother, now an old woman, was greatly worried by the grim prospects her son faced and went with one of the neighborhood women to the Carmen church to make a vow so that Johnny's little pine table would be traded in.

The suffering in his soul yielded—as does everything—with the passage of time, and John serenely continued his work. López, the experienced invoice clerk, would from time to time seek to enter into conversation with Johnny but would not receive more than a monosyllable in answer. The work became increasingly monotonous. As the days went by, more piston rings, more shock absorbers, more air filters were sold, and John could not lose one minute of time. The invoices were no longer done on white paper, as they had been in Gorostizaga's time. The company renovation had brought with it considerable changes, and invoices were now done on yellow paper, in quadruplicate, and it was necessary to press down very hard with the pencil.

The summer heat, which had always depressed him so much, now began to be harder to bear, almost tragic, especially in that little corner he worked in, with no ventilation, without even one miserable window. He was now close to fifty, and the thumb of his right hand was deformed into one enormous callus.

He rarely passed the time of day with his fellow clerks. At times he would think of Gorostizaga and the Brazilian woman with affection. He recalled that Gorostizaga had spoken to him about the Peñarol soccer team and that the Brazilian had told him that what he needed was a woman. He remembered both of them as legendary and kindly figures of the past. "How different Gorostizaga and the Brazilian woman were from these obnoxious loudmouths!" he would think. He would peek at López' desk out of the corner of his eye and squirm with displeasure.

One night, while in bed and staring at the ceiling, he made up his mind to speak with old Valbuena and ask for the desk that was his due. As soon as he arrived at the office the next day, Johnny went to see him. He was in a high bed, covered with bedclothes as voluminous as a tent; one could hardly glimpse his enormous aquiline nose trying to emerge. It was then that he learned that Valbuena, who had just turned sixty-five, had resolved to resign as Sales Manager of Mercanti, Inc. He chatted briefly with Valbuena's wife, old Mercanti's eldest daughter, and with an unmarried niece, and then said goodbye and left.

Valbuena's replacement was a certain Mr. Irigoyen, husband of the sister-in-law of Mercanti's eldest son. Johnny knew him by sight and would sometimes say hello, but did not dare to bring up the subject of the table with him. He decided to wait a few months. During this period of time he felt at ease; the postponement of confrontation provided him with a respite from tension.

Irigoyen withdrew from the firm toward the beginning of the 1960s. Later it was learned that he had a profound parting of the ways with the Mercantis, and that he had come into several million pesos through some kind of sleight-of-hand.

Johnny, who at that time was trying to get up the nerve to speak to Irigoyen about the table and about the necessity for exchanging it, experienced a sudden sense of freedom. The definitive suspension of his petition had the effect of removing an enormous weight from his shoulders, especially because he found it painful to touch on this matter with his superiors.

He bided his time. In 1962 his mother fell ill; she was almost seventy-five years old. The poor thing was placed in the sanatorium for quite a period of time, and later in a private hospital on the Avenida Agraciada because Johnny was not able to care for her.

The unfortunate woman died in January 1963. The weather was infernally hot and Johnny suffered doubly. A few days later the full impact of his situation struck home. He was completely alone in that big old house on the corner of Simón Bolívar and Charrúa. Chacho, Doña Alicia's little lap dog, had followed his mistress almost immediately to the other world. The house was empty, bereft of all human warmth. The Chinese vases, the conventional landscape paintings, the Louis XV furniture, the lamps, the mirrors, the clocks... These things meant absolutely nothing to him now. They had been removed from any context. They were a world of mute, inexpressive, uncongenial objects. He looked at them but they did not look back at him. It had not always been so; they used to be different. His mother used to infuse everything with life, with affection, with love.

Johnny continued to lead the same kind of life as before. He would leave home to go to the office, and would leave the office to return home; this routine continued without interruption. At noon he now ate at a lunch counter on the Avenida 18 de Julio, while in the evening he had his supper at some sordid little diner on Rivera Street, a block from Pocitos Station. At home there was little else for him to do but to look at the objects his mother used to look at, and to think about her. By now he had almost completely forgotten about exchanging his little table for a real desk.

One afternoon in April 1966, one of Mercanti's sons stopped at his office. It was the eldest son, already over eighty, who practically never left the house anymore. He asked Johnny how it was possible for him to work at that narrow and uncomfortable little table. Tito Mercanti was right, of course; Johnny had been working with his face to that inexpressive wall for a mere thirty-eight years now. Emotion welled up in Johnny and prevented him from expressing his feelings. All he could manage was a slight movement of his head, which Mercanti interpreted as lack of interest.

Several days later they hired a new invoice clerk. They provided him with a modern desk as well as a very comfortable swivel chair with arms, upholstered in leather. Johnny could not manage anything more than a barely civil greeting to the new clerk.

Months passed, and the cataracts which had been threatening his vision for some time now prevented him from performing his work properly. It was suggested that he retire. The new office manager told him he did not turn out enough work, that he was making too many errors, and that the best thing was for him to retire. He left his post on March 31. On April first—the next day—he stopped in at Mercanti, Inc. to pick up some certificates he needed and to take with him the photograph of the victorious Peñarol team of 1938. While he was there, he looked in at his old office. They had already hired some young kid to take his place. The new boy resembled the Johnny of almost forty years earlier. Except that this one had his own beautiful oak desk. The little table, Lopéz told him, had been sent to the warehouse to be converted into firewood. After all, it was so old and dilapidated that it wasn't fit to be used any more.

As he went down the staircase leading to the main floor, he heard his name being called. "Mr. Hernández, Mr. Hernández," the new kid in invoicing was calling, "you forgot your picture of Gardel."

Johnny took the picture, put it in his pocket and went out into the street without uttering a word.